MAGIC
BOUND
WOLF

RAYNA TYLER

NOLA ROBERTSON

ALSO BY RAYNA TYLER

Seneca Falls Shifters

Tempting the Wild Wolf
Captivated by the Cougar
Enchanting the Bear
Enticing the Wolf
Teasing the Tiger

Ketaurran Warriors

Jardun's Embrace
Khyron's Claim
Zaedon's Kiss
Rygael's Reward
Logan's Allure
Garyck's Gift

Crescent Canyon Shifters

Engaging His Mate
Impressing His Mate
Embracing His Mate

Bradshaw Bears

Bear Appeal

City Lights Shifters

Magic Bound Wolf

CHAPTER ONE

"You're not hearing me, Rand."

Of course, Phelan Rand could hear him. Hell, half of Las Vegas probably heard him. The bear shifter was bellowing so loud, Phelan's cell phone was vibrating. Besides, ignoring wasn't the same as not hearing, was it?

"You *will* be working as undercover security at the Fox and Hound for the next week. The Kerns are having some theft problems, and I expect you to take care of it." Brock Quinn, the commander of the Vegas Special Investigation Division, paused for a moment, then continued. "Before you start to argue, let me make myself extremely clear. That was an *order*, not a request." The call disconnected, and Phelan growled, tossing the offending phone across the seat of his truck. Sometimes his boss could be a royal pain in the ass. Tonight was no exception.

Phelan was a detective, damn it. He should be involved with murder investigations, not wasting his time guarding a casino. He'd worked eight years in the San Diego homicide division dealing with thieves, murderers, and rapists before transferring less than a year ago to the special branch of law enforcement specifically created to deal with any crimes involving people who weren't completely human.

For some reason, Vegas attracted them in large numbers. Quite a few of the businesses on or near the strip either catered to, or were owned by, one type of shifter or another. That didn't include the handful of magicians and psychics who either performed in visiting shows or had taken up residence in the city. Though their presence wasn't advertised, some humans were aware of their existence. For the most part, they coexisted without too many problems.

Maintaining that coexistence and ensuring the safety of the general public was the main reason the division had been created. Phelan had taken the job with the special unit to advance his career, not hinder it. Being pulled off this case was a blow to his ego, made him feel like a rookie again, and was really insulting.

If that wasn't bad enough, this particular assignment was going to cause him a huge problem. A problem he didn't care to discuss with anyone, especially not his partner and pack mate, Ryland Kern. Working at the casino meant being around Tessa. Ryland's half-sister was the most enticing female he'd ever met. The petite she-wolf had the most amazing pair of dark eyes, an unusual smoky shade. She'd filled every sexual fantasy he'd imagined since he'd met her, which was the equivalent of six months, two days, and however many hours ago. Not that he'd been pathetic enough to keep track.

The fact that she was his new alpha's niece only made it worse and put her in the top ten spots on his off-limits list. From what he'd observed, and he'd observed a lot, most of the males in Tessa's family were more than a little protective of her.

Seeing her at the monthly pack meetings was one thing. He could keep his distance and go home to an ice-cold shower. A week of being in the same building with her for hours, catching her scent, and knowing there was nothing he could do about it was going to be torment. He'd rather be beaten over the head with a lead pipe than have to endure the temptation of the one woman he desired and knew he could never have.

Along with reminders of Tessa came his wolf's constant yearnings and insistence to ardently pursue the deliciously sexy woman. For some reason, the animal had made up its mind that Tessa belonged to them. He wanted to mate her, to claim her. Even now he pushed at Phelan to go after what he thought was his.

Ignoring his wolf's urgings, he focused his thoughts on the newly reported murder, the reason he'd driven to the north end of the city in the first place. Technically, he wasn't supposed to know anything about the crime, but Ryland always managed to keep him well informed. He was the best partner Phelan had ever had and another reason he kept his distance from Tessa. Dating Ryland's sister might strain their working relationship.

This was the third homicide case he'd been pulled off in the last month, and it was starting to grate. Temporarily reassigned or not, he'd already responded to Ryland's call. The least he could do was put in an appearance and support his partner. If he happened to gather some information about the case while he was there, even better.

Phelan knew the minute he arrived on the crime scene that Brock would hear about it and he risked a shouting match, one where he did most of the listening. Right now he was too irritated to care. Any aggravation he caused his boss far outweighed the prospect of receiving another shitty assignment.

He slid out of the truck and slammed the door. The evening air was warm, thick with humidity from an earlier rain storm, and coated his skin with a thin layer of moisture. Reaching for some much-needed calm, he tipped his head back and glanced at the brightly lit sky. Fragments of darkness speckled the background beyond the array of light from the hotels, casinos, and flashing marquees. It always amazed him how busy and alive the city seemed long after the sun had set.

He turned away from the main strip and headed down the sidewalk leading to the rear of the Woodland Acres Hotel and Casino. The impressive ten-story complex designed to replicate a fantasy forest comprised an entire city block and was owned by Grant Fowler, a powerful grizzly bear shifter.

Having met the man on several different occasions, Phelan knew he'd be upset and difficult to deal with once he discovered a murder victim had been found near the edge of his property. If he was working the case, handling Grant would have been his responsibility since Ryland had no patience for him. Now that he was off the case, his partner would happily direct Grant and his complaints to Brock. He couldn't hold back a grin as he imagined how that conversation would go.

Reaching the end of the block and the entrance to a shadowed alleyway, he found a crowd of onlookers being kept back by several local patrol officers. After showing his badge and receiving an approving nod from one of the men, he ducked under the strip of yellow plastic strung across the opening.

He'd taken only a few steps into the confined area when the heavy stench of blood, stagnant water, and death accosted his wolf's heightened sense of smell. He breathed through his mouth to minimize the burn to his nostrils and reduce his animal's agitation.

So far the only detail he'd received was that the victim was a woman and had been found by one of the hotel's employees who had stepped outside to smoke for his break. There were numerous plastic bags, along with shredded produce boxes, sitting on the concrete slab next to an overflowing Dumpster. Someone had tossed her body on top of the pile of trash.

He spotted Ryland leaning against the side of a police cruiser, exuding his usual calm and patience as he waited for the medical examiner's staff to finish their work. After giving Phelan a curt nod, he returned his attention to the scene, or rather Marina, the beautiful human investigator. The first time Phelan met her, she'd made it abundantly clear that she didn't want them anywhere near the scene until her team had finished processing the area.

Besides being thorough and good at her job, Marina was straightforward and didn't cut anyone any slack. Though Ryland had tried to conceal his interest, it hadn't taken Phelan long to figure out his friend lusted after the hot and sexy redhead. He didn't have to be a detective to sense the sexual tension and chemistry that flared between the two of them every time they got within a few feet of each other.

Marina wore a baggy pair of the standard white coveralls she used to protect her clothing while she worked. She kept her movements slow and careful, making sure not to disrupt anything as she snapped photographs of the body and the surrounding area.

Phelan had been trying for months to get his partner to open up and tell him why he wouldn't ask her out. No matter how much he teased Ryland, the words "It's complicated" followed by long stretches of silence were the only responses he received.

"Find out anything yet?" Phelan stopped a foot away from Ryland and leaned against the car door.

"No. The ME's team arrived about fifteen minutes ago, so we're waiting." Ryland grabbed a Styrofoam cup off the hood and handed it to him. "Thought you might need this. It's probably going to be a long night."

Longer than you think. An image of Tessa flashed through his mind again as he took the cup. "Thanks." Before he'd moved to Vegas, his coffee intake rarely made it past eleven o'clock in the morning. Lately, he'd adapted to Ryland's schedule of drinking the strong brew at all hours of the day and sometimes during the night.

One quick sniff told him the coffee was black, his usual preference. He would have gagged if he'd gotten Ryland's by mistake. The man loved to load his drink down with cream and sugar, something Phelan had discovered during an early morning investigation when their drinks had accidentally gotten switched. He swallowed a long swig, reveling in the warm burn as the caffeine-laced liquid rolled across his tongue.

"You didn't look too happy when you arrived." Ryland shot him a studious glance. "Did Brock pull you off the case and give you another crappy assignment?"

Phelan nodded and gripped the cup tighter. "It's been eight months already." *Eight really long months.* "How long can he hold a grudge?" Hearing the foam crackle, he relaxed his grip, preferring not to wear the drink on his clothes.

"You did sleep with his niece. And if I remember correctly, I warned you she would be trouble and not to mess with her. Bears are mean and surly when it comes to family." Ryland grinned and gave him one of his smug I-told-you-so looks before taking another swallow of his own drink.

"Yeah, yeah, I got it already." Too bad Ryland had neglected to mention Tanzy's relationship to their boss at the time he was giving him advice. If he had, Phelan would have thought twice about going home with her. He growled and glared at his partner, irritated by the constant reminder about the indiscretion he'd made shortly after transferring to the city. The stupid mistake had transformed his work life into a miserable existence, and thinking about it wasn't helping his already foul mood.

Tanzy, the woman in question, was a bartender at the Firelite bar, a local shifter hangout. He and Ryland had solved their first case together and had stopped by the bar to celebrate. The case had been a double homicide involving some casino winnings and a pissed-off wolf. One drink had turned into five, then some harmless flirting, mostly on Tanzy's part, had turned into an invitation for sex.

Tanzy had made it clear she was only interested in

playing for one night, and being new to the city, he and his wolf were happy to oblige. He was, after all, male, and at the time, in need of some sexual relief. Not long after that, he'd met Tessa and his sex life had become nonexistent. He'd had more than one fantasy that involved her naked underneath him, writhing and moaning, which pretty much ruined his interest in any other females.

"What does Brock want you to do this time? Walk a beat with the locals, or wait, I know." Ryland chuckled and tapped his arm. "He has you working purse-snatcher duty on the strip again."

A warning growl rumbled from Phelan's chest. He particularly didn't want to hear about his last assignment. The assignment where he'd ended up with a black eye. An elderly woman from Idaho had smacked him in the head when he tried to keep her purse from being stolen. The damage to his pride had lasted a lot longer than the bruises. He was still getting grief about it from the other detectives.

"Screw you, Kern." He extended the middle finger of his right hand along the edge of his cup as he took another drink. "This assignment is courtesy of Logan. I've been ordered to work security at the casino until the end of the week."

"What's going on at the casino?" By the way Ryland's voice pitched higher and his shoulders tensed, Phelan guessed this was the first he'd heard about any problems at the casino.

"I guess he's had some thefts and wants me to investigate."

"Why is he getting you involved? He usually handles those types of issues himself or has someone in the family take care of it."

"There are a lot of shows scheduled for this week." With all the extra people visiting the city, their department was going to be putting in some extra hours. "Maybe he's too busy and doesn't have time to mess with it." *Or maybe*

7

Brock volunteered my services just to be an asshole. Logan wouldn't be able to ask for Ryland's help because most of the employees knew him. If it was someone who worked at the casino, they'd immediately be suspicious. Since Phelan tended to stay away from the casino, it made him the perfect candidate.

The fact that Logan and Brock were close friends and Phelan was currently on his boss's don't-screw-with-my-niece list probably had something to do with it. After his ordeal of meeting Tanzy, Phelan wondered how many other guys had ended up on the same list.

"Logan have any ideas who it is?" Ryland asked.

"Brock didn't say." Actually, Phelan had been too busy trying to ignore the roaring to pay attention to what the overbearing black bear had to say. He drained the last of his coffee and set the cup on the hood of the vehicle.

"I can't figure out who'd be stupid enough to steal from my family. The shifters would know better, and the humans on his staff are loyal and have been with him a long time." Ryland shifted, leaning more of his weight on the vehicle so he could cross his legs at the ankles. "Unless it's someone new to the city like that guy we caught a month ago who was stealing from the casinos."

Phelan remembered the incident quite well. A twenty-two-year-old human male had made the mistake of picking pockets in full view of the security cameras. Needless to say, when Logan was finished with the kid, he'd found a new profession, and they hadn't seen him in the casino since. "Hopefully, it won't take me long to find out who's behind the thefts." Not that it would shorten the amount of time Phelan had to spend at the casino or have him back solving crimes anytime soon. Brock had specified a week and no doubt meant it.

"Looks like they're finishing up." Phelan noticed Stan, another member of Marina's team, setting his equipment in the back of the medical examiner's van.

Marina carefully returned her camera to its case. She

unzipped her coveralls and pushed them down to her ankles, then stepped out to reveal a hot-pink spaghetti-strap dress clinging to her petite form. The fabric barely reached mid-thigh and showed off a pair of long, evenly tanned legs. She was definitely overdressed, or underdressed, depending on how you looked at it.

The woman had a lot to offer in the hot-and-sexy department, but not enough to draw Phelan's interest. He couldn't, however, say the same for Ryland, who intently watched her movements. His friend tensed, then released a low growl as he pushed away from the car.

She replaced the plain white slip-on boots with a pair of fancy black stilettos. Since it was nearing eight on a Friday night, Phelan had a suspicion she'd been torn away from an important engagement.

Phelan couldn't resist getting a little payback for his partner's earlier comments. "Damn, Marina sure looks good tonight. Looks like she might have been on a date before she got called into work."

As he'd expected, Ryland snarled, "Shut up, *Rand*."

Whether intentional or not, she drew the attention of every male in the general vicinity of the crime scene. Unaware that their conversation could be easily overheard, one of the officers manning the entrance elbowed his partner and said, "Now that's a nice piece of ass. I wouldn't mind tapping that."

"Don't." Phelan clamped a hand on Ryland's arm when he took a step forward as if he were going to pounce on the younger man.

"I won't kill him." Ryland shrugged away from Phelan's grip and stalked toward the officer with the stealth of a predator.

Slightly worried his partner might lose it, Phelan kept a close watch, prepared to intervene if necessary. Any other time, if there hadn't been a lot of other humans around, he'd gladly gone after the man himself for making the derogatory remark. No woman should have to put up with that kind of crap.

The two men had been too busy chuckling between themselves to notice Ryland until he was standing three feet away from them. One of the officers glanced at him, his smile quickly fading. He slapped the man who'd made the comment in the chest with the back of his hand, gaining his attention.

His gaze landed on Ryland, and whatever he saw had him swallowing hard and taking a nervous step backward. Phelan scented his fear and wouldn't be surprised if the man ended up peeing himself.

"Any more comments about her ass and I'm going to rip off your balls and feed them to you." Ryland's voice came out intimidating, low, and borderline feral. "Are we clear?"

Shock and fear flickered across the man's face, his skin paling to a ghostly white. "Yeah…" He took another step back and protectively covered his groin.

"Good." Ryland quickly dismissed them and returned to stand next to Phelan.

Marina might be human, but noise in the narrow alleyway carried. When she cocked her head in their direction, Phelan knew the interaction between the men had drawn her attention. She narrowed her dark eyes and strode toward them, her bright auburn curls bouncing with every click the two-inch heels made against the concrete. She reached them a few seconds after Ryland got back to the car.

She directed her concerned gaze at Ryland. "What's going on?"

"Nothing."

Marina slipped her hands to her hips. "It didn't sound like nothing."

Phelan would probably regret it, but he could still sense Ryland's anger and decided to draw her attention away from him. "You look nice tonight, Marina. I hope being called into work didn't mess up your evening." He used the best apologetic tone he could muster.

Her gaze softened. "Dreadful dinner party at my sister's."

"Not a hot date," Phelan teased.

"No, no date." She laughed. "I was actually happy for the interruption."

"Can you tell us anything about the victim?" Ryland interrupted. "Do you know who she was?"

Marina's smile faded. "No identification yet."

"How about the cause of death?" Ryland asked.

"I'm afraid you'll have to wait for the ME's report." Marina blew out a breath. "Whoever did this went to a lot of trouble to conceal her identity. She's been tortured pretty badly. A lot of claw marks and bruising all over her body."

"Are you thinking a shifter was responsible?" Phelan asked.

"It certainly looks like a possibility." Marina cringed, her voice barely above a whisper. "There's a strange green tint to her skin. I've never seen anything like it. Maybe some kind of magic. Again, we won't know until we've had a chance to run some tests."

"Mind if we do a little scenting?" Marina was one of the few humans working in the ME's office who knew they were shifters and would understand Phelan's reason for asking. He was an excellent tracker. If there was even a hint of the killer on the woman's skin, he'd be able to detect it.

"I don't think it will do any good. Whoever did this knew what they were doing. They made sure she was covered with trash to hide their scent."

"Hey, Marina, you ready to go?" Stan had placed the woman's body on a gurney and was loading it into the back of the van.

"Be right there." She glanced over her shoulder and waved at Stan, then turned her attention back to them. "I need to go." Her gaze locked on Ryland when she spoke.

11

"You guys be careful. Whoever did this is one vicious son of a bitch." She spun on her heel and walked away.

Phelan smacked Ryland's shoulder.

"What was that for?" Ryland snarled.

"What is it with you two, and when are you going to ask her out?" Phelan asked.

"I told you. It's complicated," Ryland replied defensively, never taking his eyes off Marina until she slipped into the passenger seat and closed the vehicle door.

Someone picked that moment to call Phelan. He slid his phone out of his pocket, read the message on the display, and groaned.

"Logan?" Ryland asked.

"Yes. He's wondering why I'm not there yet."

"Better get going before he calls Brock and asks him what the happened to you. I'll call you as soon as I hear anything new about the victim."

"Thanks. Appreciate it." Phelan liked that about his partner. No matter how much shit his boss gave him, Ryland still went out of his way to keep him in the loop on their cases.

CHAPTER TWO

Just another day in paradise... Tessa was certain whoever dreamed up that saying had never worked a double shift at the Fox and Hound.

Clutching a damp cloth in one hand and a brown plastic serving tray in the other, she worked her way toward a recently vacated table in the small dining area opposite the bar. The remainder of the tables were occupied by customers who were snacking and drinking, or who had stopped to enjoy the ambiance of the surrounding casino.

Having worked at the family-owned business for a number of years, she barely registered the familiar bells, whistles, and musical noises made by the multiple rows of slot machines, or the occasional clank from coins dropping into metal trays, the whoops and hollers of winners, and the deep moans and groans of the not-so-lucky losers.

She might not be able to shift, but her wolf still had an acute sense of smell and hearing. Tessa didn't need to turn around to know her uncle had followed her from the bar or that he was standing behind her with his arms crossed. She imagined his crystal-blue eyes, the same luminescent shade as some of the other males in her family, were expectantly staring at her back.

"Tessa?" Logan's deep, husky rumble rolled over her, along with his anxiety. He was a dominant wolf and naturally exuded power whether he meant to or not. And right now it was directed at her and demanding her full attention.

"Whatever it is, the answer is no." Refusing to face him, she braced for the discussion she knew she wasn't going to like. With a heavy sigh, she picked up the empty drink glasses from the table and placed them on the tray. Afterward, she wiped the smoothly lacquered wood grain surface with the cloth.

"I haven't even told you what I want."

Want, not need. Definitely a bad sign. "Still no."

"As your al…"

More than a little annoyed at his persistence, she swung around and glared at him. "Tell me you weren't going to play the alpha card on me." Yep, as predicted, his arms were wrapped tightly across his broad chest, flexed against the short sleeves of his blue cotton shirt. A few golden strands touched his forehead but didn't hide the deep frown creasing his slightly darker brows.

All the Kern males were ripped mountains of muscle, and her uncle was no exception. Sometimes she wondered if being intimidating and taking up someone's personal space wasn't a prerequisite for all the men in her family. Not that it bothered her any since she'd grown used to it. Being five or so inches shorter than their six-foot-plus heights didn't bother her. After many years of practice, she could hold her own with every one of them.

"I would never." He clenched his jaw, red spreading along his cheeks.

"Really?" She bit back an amused smile, propped the edge of the tray against her hip, and patiently waited for him to explain what was so important.

"I need you to work the blackjack tables until the end of your shift."

She groaned, not bothering to hide her exasperation. "You know I hate dealing blackjack." Actually, she wasn't thrilled about working any of the gambling tables. It meant staying in one spot for an extended period of time. She preferred working the bar or serving drinks in the slot machine area. It gave her the chance to move around and kept her wolf from growing restless or feeling trapped. A downside to not being able to shift.

"I know, but you'll still do it for me, right?" Logan's question sounded more like a command than a request. It didn't take him long to realize she wasn't going to budge if he pushed. "Aurelia called in sick, and I'm already shorthanded." He unfolded his arms and softened his expression. "Please, I need your help."

Male shifters did not beg under any circumstances, especially the pack's alpha. Manipulate, cajole, bully, yes. Beg, no. His strained efforts to do something that went against every one of his natural instincts almost had her feeling sorry for him. Almost.

This was the second time in a week her younger cousin had missed her shift. If she found out that Aurelia had blown off work again to hang out with her worthless couldn't-hold-a-job-for-a-week boyfriend, Tessa was going to kill her. Or at the very least put permanent hair color— maybe a shade of green this time—in her shampoo. The last time she'd gotten even with Aurelia, she'd had to go to a professional hairdresser to get rid of the purple streaks.

It was the middle of June, and there were at least three trade shows and conferences scheduled for the next week. It pissed Tessa off that Aurelia was pulling this shit when the hotel was booked to capacity and the casino was overloaded with visitors. The additional income was nice, but as a family member, it meant she was expected to put in more hours than normal.

Logan scratched the stubble along his chin. "What if I paid you double-time for the entire shift?"

"I don't know." She clamped her lips together tightly,

hiding a smile and trying for feigned indifference. Her uncle was a shrewd and successful businessman. He had to be desperate if he was willing to pay for the favor. "Doesn't seem worth the trouble. I can make more tips serving drinks." She kept her gaze locked with his and knew the minute he slid his hand through his hair that she had him.

"Fine, I'll also throw in two paid days off, but you can't use them until after this week." In other words, he still expected her to continue working her backside off.

"Deal," she said and handed him the tray. She should have held out for an entire week but didn't want to push her luck. Besides, the way things were going, she figured it wouldn't be long before he was asking for more favors. If she worked it right, she might be able to get the extra time off anyway.

"You're the best." He leaned forward, kissed her on the cheek, and headed for the bar.

Sure, he says that now. She'd bet he wouldn't be saying that to her in another hour when she was cranky and making someone cry. She glanced at the metal replica of a fox hanging on the wall behind the bar. The clock in its center showed the time as five minutes after nine. Rolling the stiffness out of her shoulders, she inhaled deeply and headed for the blackjack area. Less than three hours to go before her shift was done. She could do this. *What can possibly go wrong?*

\#

Phelan leaned against the shiny chrome railing separating the bar from the gaming area in the Fox and Hound. He spotted Tessa walking through the casino, and his chest constricted, forcing his blood to beat a rapid tempo in his heart. The same rapid tempo he'd experienced the first time he'd met her and every time he'd seen her since.

Even wearing a work uniform, the sexy shifter was stunning. Her eyes shimmered a shade of smoky quartz that would make the most expensive gemstones jealous. When she turned and headed through the slot machine area, he caught a glimpse of her back. She'd secured her long hair at the nape, the dark silky strands, naturally highlighted with copper streaks, bounced playfully against the middle of her back.

He lowered his gaze, admiring her long, slender legs and the way the fabric of her short skirt clung tightly to one of the finest asses he'd ever seen. She had curves in all the right places, made him hard, and raised havoc with his wolf's senses.

Once again he found himself wishing she wasn't his partner's sister or Logan's only niece. If things were different, he'd make a move on the beautiful woman. And do what, he chastised himself. Get her in his bed for one night and screw her until he got her out of his system. Tessa wasn't a one-night stand kind of woman. There was more to his attraction to her than he wanted to admit. He had a feeling one night would never be enough.

Mate. His wolf growled, making his presence known, urging him to go after her. It wasn't possible, and Phelan wanted to argue the point with the stubborn animal but knew he wouldn't listen. Shifters were wired to recognize their mates. If Tessa was intended to be his, wouldn't he know it?

He stared at Tessa until she disappeared into a crowd of people. As much as he wanted to take his wolf's advice and traipse after her, he couldn't. He was here to do a job. Hopefully, the sooner he completed his task, the sooner he could get out of here and away from the tempting she-wolf.

He caught sight of Logan carrying a tray and ducking behind the bar. Knowing he couldn't put it off any longer, he walked around a group of tables and approached the long counter.

"About time you showed up." Logan frowned and glanced at the drink he was preparing.

"Got tied up." Alpha or not, unless Logan pressed him for more information, Phelan had no intention of offering a detailed explanation of his whereabouts.

"How is my nephew?" Logan set the drink on the counter and reached for another glass. "I assume you being held up had something to do with the recent murder near the Woodlands."

How does he always know these things? This wasn't the first time Logan had astonished him by knowing confidential information. Since he'd asked about Ryland, he scratched his partner off as the source.

Phelan thought about refuting the insinuation. The denial was on the tip of his tongue. Instead, he remained silent.

"I'll take that as a yes." Logan raised a thick brow and gave him the same all-knowing look he used to get from his father when he was younger. It was either a parent thing, an alpha thing, or a mixture of both. Phelan still hadn't decided.

Best to change the subject back to work. "Want to fill me in on what you need, why I'm here?"

"Brock's probably already told you I've been having some theft problems."

"He mentioned it." Phelan rubbed his chin.

"Whoever is stealing from the customers knows exactly where all the security cameras are located, and so far, they've managed to avoid being seen." Logan topped off the drink by slipping a partially sliced strawberry on the edge of the glass rim.

"Do you think it could be an employee?"

"Most of the people who work for me are either family or have worked here for a long time. I would hate to think I have someone in-house that I can't trust." Logan set both drinks on a tray, then motioned to a waitress at the other end of the bar. "This is ready to go."

"Thanks." After picking up the tray, the young brunette smiled sweetly at Phelan and headed in the direction of the tables.

Once they were alone, Phelan asked, "Is there anyone you fired lately? Someone who might hold a grudge."

"No one comes to mind." Logan gripped the edge of the counter until white appeared on his knuckles. "I may trust my family and the employees but that doesn't mean I expect you to do the same. I want you to treat everyone as a suspect during your investigation until you can rule them out."

"Anyplace you'd like me to start?" Phelan didn't think he could admire and respect Logan any more than he already did. Adhering to a higher standard and holding everyone accountable, including his own family, was one of the things that made the man such a good alpha.

Some of the employees belonged to the pack. And stealing from Logan's customers was the same as stealing from the alpha. Phelan didn't want to think about what would happen if the person responsible was a member. Pack hierarchy overruled local law enforcement. Logan would have to issue judgment, and the penalty would be severe.

"Can you go up to room 314 and speak with Mrs. Barnett? I have assured her we'll do everything we can to recover her missing jewelry. I'm sure I don't need to tell you we need to catch whoever is doing this quickly." Logan picked up a slip of paper the waitress had dropped on the counter before rushing off.

"I'll see what I can do."

"Oh, and Phelan." He'd made it only a few steps before Logan called out to him.

He stopped and glanced over his shoulder. "Yeah?"

"I heard about Tanzy. Solve this for me, and I'll see what I can do to get Brock off your back."

Was there anyone in the city who didn't know about his damned indiscretion? Phelan turned and headed in the direction of the lobby and the main elevators.

CHAPTER THREE

Two more hours, two more hours, two more hours. The chant wasn't working to ease Tessa's stress. She still couldn't believe she'd let Logan talk her into working the blackjack table. Hopefully, having two full days off from work would be worth it. Her thoughts drifted to the things she planned to do with her time. Maybe she'd go to the movies, spend the day shopping, or simply lounge around in a nightshirt all day. She'd been working a lot of hours lately, so whatever she decided to do would be leisurely and require a minimal amount of effort.

A gruff groan from an elderly man snapped her back to reality. After quickly apologizing for bumping into him, she made her way across the main floor of the casino. Besides all the humans, there were a few different types of shifters in the crowd she passed through. Tessa scented a couple of bears and wolves, an occasional fox, and one, maybe two, cougars.

By the time she reached her table, a gnawing ache thrummed across her forehead, threatening the onset of a massive migraine. The raised noise level from all the conversations, coins clanging, bells, and whistles was wearing down the barrier she used to shroud her empathetic powers. Powers she'd received from a magician father who'd bailed on her the first chance he got. All thanks to her mother's inability to commit to any kind of relationship for more than five minutes, including the one with her daughter.

Most shifters waited for their mates, the one person they were meant to spend the rest of their lives with. For some reason, Margery Kern Shaw refused to admit there was such a thing. It explained why she was currently working on husband number four.

Tessa knew for a fact that finding a mate was possible. She had several friends who'd found their match and were living happy lives. Something she longed for but knew would never happen. Her mother constantly reminded her that she was too different and no wolf would want her, especially an intended mate.

Tess refused to end up like her mother. It was why she randomly dated, never allowing a guy to get too close, never allowing them to know about her differences.

Pushing away the thoughts that always depressed her, Tessa prepped the table for the first game. She didn't have long to wait before she was dealing cards to a newlywed couple from Dickinson, North Dakota, and two friendly and flirtatious businessmen from Los Angeles. Listening to the groups' pleasant banter kept her entertained and made the time go by faster.

She'd finished placing chips on the table for the winners when a prickly sense of wrongness skimmed across her skin. A man suddenly appeared at her side, a jackal shifter if she'd smelled correctly. The man's nearness irritated her wolf. Her animal snarled and snapped her teeth, prepared to pounce, to protect.

Even with all the different smells filling the air, Tessa's wolf should have been able to detect his presence long before he'd reached the table. Either something was seriously wrong with her ability to scent, or he'd found a way to mask his animal's odor. Something Tessa didn't think was possible.

"Such a pretty little wolf." He kept his voice low so only she could hear, then brushed his fingertips across her bare arm as he walked past her to take a seat in the available chair to her right. As he set his drink on the table, his scrutinizing gaze never wavered.

Revulsion washed through her, and she flinched and fought the urge to run. *What is a jackal doing in Kern pack territory?* The scavenger shifters were worse than hyenas—enemies to all other breeds—always encroaching on other territories.

As far as she knew, the nearest jackal pack was located in Arizona, near Kingman and the surrounding desert areas. Most of them knew better than to stray across the Nevada state line without gaining permission from an alpha. Permission she knew for a fact this guy didn't have. Logan would never allow a jackal into the city without assigning an escort and alerting the entire family of his presence.

A smirk played across his lips. Lust filled his beady dark eyes, and he lowered his gaze, scanning the length of her. His slow perusal made her skin itch. She nervously slid her hands along her short skirt, wishing the fabric stretched past her ankles.

He gave her an amused snort and licked his lips in a long, slow swipe. "Surely someone as beautiful as you will bring me good luck." His arrogant tone fell short on exuding any charm.

Tessa was used to having men, both human and shifter, hit on her, some more aggressively than others. Most nights a little friendly conversation and harmless flirting ensured she'd receive decent tips.

This guy was disgusting and vile, and his advances bordered on dangerous, which had her senses tingling and her wolf pacing. Brazenly strutting into pack territory—her family's property—proved he was either insane or extremely deadly. Tessa was betting on the latter.

The man obviously had expensive tastes. She was no expert, but the cut of his gray suit coat sat too perfectly across his broad shoulders to be anything less than hand-tailored. Beneath it he wore a blue satin shirt with the top three buttons undone to expose his chest.

It was hard not to notice the unusual silver pendant he had hanging around his neck. A large crimson stone resembling a ruby was positioned in the center and held in place by groupings of miniature talons. It might be a trick of the overhead lighting, but she'd swear the gem was glowing.

Tessa was torn between fleeing to find Logan and remaining to monitor the intruder. Her wolf wanted to stay, to protect the humans at the table. She cast a quick glance around the room, hoping someone in her family or one of the shifter employees had noticed the jackal.

Nothing. Not a wary look in her direction. Not a hint of emotional unease to indicate someone else was aware of his presence.

"Tessa. What a pretty name." His mention of her name jerked her attention back to him. Before she could ask how he knew her, she noticed him staring at the name tag pinned to her shirt below her left shoulder.

"You can call me Draven." His gaze lifted to hers and he placed a twenty-dollar bill on the table.

No, I'd rather not. She'd rather he got out of the casino, preferably the entire state. Hesitantly, she took the money and exchanged it for chips from the tray sitting in front of her.

The humans at the table might not be aware of Draven's predatory nature, but they must have sensed the threatening power pulsing off him in waves. The young groom, who'd previously been enjoying a winning streak, pulled his new bride closer and warily glanced in Draven's direction. Apparently, the businessmen had picked up on the tension, because they no longer had any interest in playful conversation.

Tessa waited for everyone to place their chips in the small circles designated for bets for the next game. Draven kept his unnerving gaze focused on her and was the last one to place two red chips on the table.

Swallowing the nervous knot constricting her throat, she placed a card faceup in front of each person who'd placed bets. She concentrated her efforts on the game, secretly hoping the jackal would lose interest and move on to another table so she could find Logan and warn him.

Once the game ended, everyone except Draven grabbed their chips and their drinks, then scurried away.

"Guess it's you and me." Draven didn't bother to hide his amusement as he watched the others disappear into the crowd. He lifted a stack of chips off the table, then released them in one unnerving click after another. "Tell me, Tessa. Are you related to the owner? To Logan Kern."

"I'm not sure that's any of your business." She eyed him suspiciously and tried not to sound confrontational. His intense stare was chipping away at her resolve to remain professional, and she wanted him to leave. "Were you going to play another game? If not, you'll need to leave to make room for others."

He glanced at the four empty seats and grinned as if guessing her bluff. "I'll play." He left the chips he'd won from the previous game on the table. "I'm enjoying the company and the view."

Back to disgusting. Her fingertips had barely touched the next card in the deck when everything around her blurred. She froze and blinked. As soon as her vision came back into focus, a sharp pain pressed against her temples. At first she thought she was experiencing a severe migraine. She'd had them before. They were a side effect of being an empath, rare but not uncommon.

The pain intensified as more pressure pushed against her mental barrier, the shield she used to block out other people's emotions. Another painful shove and a woman's voice screamed inside her head, *"Help me."*

What the heck? Tessa's pulse raced, and she grabbed the edge of the table with unsteady hands. *Brain tumor.* Margery's prophesized words taunted her. Her mother constantly ranted about all the things that could go wrong with her from having magician's blood running through her veins.

It wasn't as if Tessa had a choice in selecting her father. Normally, she ignored her mother when she raved about Thomas Shaw's long list of indiscretions and inadequacies. Over the years, she'd speculated whether or not Margery was the reason her third husband had disappeared from Tessa's life.

"Tessa, you're not hearing things and you don't have a brain tumor." She heard the woman's frustrated sigh. *"My name is Nira, and I'm quite real. You are the only one who can hear me."*

Great. Her insanity had a name. *"If I'm not losing my mind, and you are real…"* Not that Tessa was convinced. She glanced at Draven to confirm if what Nira had said was true and found him leering at a passing waitress, completely oblivious to their conversation. *"How are you able to get inside my head?"*

This was getting too weird. Tessa had been able to sense other people's emotions since she was a child. Only a few close members of her family knew she possessed the power. She'd never been able to telepathically converse with anyone before. She took a deep breath and reinforced her shield. Didn't a person need to be nearby in order for them to link with someone else's mind?

She glanced around the casino. People were placing bets, ordering drinks, or cheering for the occasional winner. Her coworkers were busy doing their jobs. She didn't see anyone close by who remotely resembled someone who could slip into her thoughts. Not that she had any idea what a person would look like when they performed telepathy.

"I'm a Druid descendant with magical powers. Telepathy is one of my gifts."

"As in fairy?"

"Forest fairy to be exact."

Tessa couldn't help being astonished by the revelation. She knew there were magical beings in the world. She was living proof. Yet to have a mental conversation with one was a bit overwhelming.

"Whenever you're ready," Draven snarled, then drained the last of his drink.

"Oh, sorry." Tessa ignored the conversation in her mind and concentrated on dealing the next hand. She laid two cards faceup on the table next to Draven's bet, then placed a card faceup in front of her tray and slid the fourth facedown underneath it.

The pain in Tessa's head was getting worse. She was exhausted from being on her feet most of the day, getting crankier by the minute, and absolutely not in the mood for games. While she waited for Draven to decide whether he wanted to hold or take another card, she focused her attention back to Nira. *"I'm not sure how they do things where you're from, but invading someone's mind without permission is rude. I would appreciate it if you got out of my head."* Like right now, but she kept that thought to herself.

Draven flicked his fingers, indicating he wanted another card. When Tessa didn't respond right away, he snapped his fingers. "Hey sweetheart, you sleeping or what? I signaled for you to hit me." He shot her an irritated glare, and a sneer contorted his face.

"Sorry." She wanted to hit him all right, but not with a card. Searching for calm, she dug her fingernails into the palm of her clenched fist. The last thing she needed was to piss off the jackal. Gaining her composure, she pulled a card from the deck and laid it on the table.

Tessa dealt another game for Draven and thought Nira was done messing with her head until she heard her pleading voice. *"Please. You don't understand. You're the only one who can help me."* Nira sounded as if she'd been crying, and her desperation pulled at Tessa's heart.

"Help you how?" What could possibly be so bad that Nira had to solicit aid using her mind? Tessa placed Draven's winnings on the table and waited to see if he was going to play another game.

"I'm being held prisoner by Draven Thorn, the man sitting at your table."

"What?" Shocked, Tess blurted the question out loud.

Draven quirked his brow in an inquisitive manner but didn't say anything.

"Nira, what do you mean you're being held prisoner. Where?" Did Draven have her locked up somewhere, maybe one of their hotel rooms?

"My essence is trapped in the pendant around his neck."

Tessa glanced at the red gem. *"How is that even possible?"* Of all the scenarios she could imagine, that was definitely not what she expected to hear. The night had gone from strange to majorly bizarre.

"I'm not sure. My memory is a little fuzzy." Nira sniffled. *"I do know that if I don't reconnect with my body before sunset on the solstice in two days, I will be bound to him forever."*

"Why would he want to do that?" Scratch bizarre. What Tessa was hearing sounded too surreal to be believable. Too afraid Draven might sense her fear, she tried not to stare at him. She was relieved when he signaled the waitress serving at the adjacent table. As soon as he had the woman's attention, he held up his empty glass and motioned for her to bring him another drink. She must have served him before, because she gave him a brief nod, then headed in the direction of the bar.

"He's using dark magic, and if he absorbs my powers…he'll be more powerful than any other alpha. He'll be able to do whatever he wants, and no one will be able to stop him."

"Crap." Tessa wanted to use a stronger curse word but didn't want to offend Nira. Other than their ability to shift into a dangerous animal, jackals didn't possess magical powers. If what Nira said was true, and Tessa still had some lingering doubts, then this was bad. Very bad.

A jackal with power—any kind of power—was a threat to all the shifters, not just her family. Tessa couldn't walk away. She needed to find a way to help, which meant she needed to keep Draven at the table as long as possible. *"Is there someone I can contact. A friend, family?"* Surely Nira wasn't in the city by herself.

Tessa forced a smile and asked Draven, "Are you ready for another game?"

"Why not?" He grinned and inclined his head, then dropped two chips into the circle on the table.

"My father is overprotective. I wanted to experience the world, so I came here alone."

Not the smartest move. Parts of the city could be dangerous to someone who didn't know what to avoid. Growing up with the dominant men in her family, Tessa understood the need for independence. *"Why contact me? I don't have any magical powers, any way to help you."* She dealt to Draven, then to herself.

"You need to get the pendant away from him and return it to my body."

At Draven's request, Tessa placed another card on the table. *"Are you kidding?"* She'd come close to asking the question out loud. *"How do you suggest I do that?"* Without being shredded to pieces. *"If, and it's an extremely big if, I manage to get the pendant, how am I supposed to find you?"*

"I don't know." Nira sobbed forlornly.

Tessa had been the recipient of Ryland's interrogation tactics since she'd turned seventeen and started dating. She tried to think of questions he would ask. *"Do you remember what you did last night? Where you went?"*

"I had some complimentary tickets, so I walked along the strip and visited different bars."

If Tessa had to guess, she'd say Nira wasn't much older than twenty-one. She wanted to scold her, tell her how stupid it was to go barhopping by herself in a strange place, but it was kind of a moot point now. *"Do you remember the last place you went?"*

"No, I'm sorry, I don't."

Since Draven had placed a hold on his cards, Tessa flipped over her hidden card, exposing the ten of diamonds. Combined with the king of spades, it gave her a total of twenty. Draven only had seventeen and lost the game, the third one in a row. Apparently, he was a sore loser, because he snarled when she removed his chips. He pressed his lips tightly together, and his pupils darkened into reflective black orbs that no longer appeared human.

Luckily, Tina, one of the waitresses, picked that moment to deliver his drink. "Thanks," he hissed and tossed a chip on her tray.

Tina took an uneasy step backward. She was human and had no idea the man she'd served was a jackal. He was showing signs of losing control of his animal. Tessa wanted to scream at her to find Logan and send him to her table, but hesitated. She was too afraid that mentioning her uncle's name would send Draven over the edge, trigger his shift, and expose their kind to the humans in the room.

Taking a sip from his new drink didn't seem to help his anger. He stared at her over the rim of the glass, his grip so tight, she could see the white straining across his knuckles. Tessa lowered her gaze to the chain around his neck and wondered how far she'd get if she grabbed the pendant and ran.

"Tessa. Something's wrong." Nira sounded on the verge of hysterics. *"My magic is fading...I..."*

"No. Nira. Wait." *Oh shit, I said that out loud.* Tessa met Draven's dark glare.

"What did you say?" His voice was a low growl, more animal than human. His lips tightened into a firm line, and sharp claws extended from his fingernails. He gripped the edge of the table, leaving deep gashes in the wood.

Tessa swallowed hard and slowly backed away from the table. There was going to be bloodshed. Going by the animalistic expression on his face, Draven planned to start with her.

CHAPTER FOUR

Phelan's meeting with Mrs. Barnett, or Elsa, as she'd insisted he call her, had been a complete waste of time. The fifty-something human female had been more interested in trying to get him between the sheets of her turned-down bed than she was in finding her stolen pearl necklace.

Supposedly she'd seen too many movies about the wild times to be had in Las Vegas and wanted to include him in her memorable moments. She'd come to the city with a few of her friends from some small town in Oklahoma—the name he couldn't recall—to have, and she quoted, an unforgettable weekend. More than once, he'd had to disengage her hands from around his neck.

Through all the mauling, he'd managed to get the answers to a couple of his questions, such as, yes, she'd worn it the night before when attending one of the shows on the strip with her friends. And yes, she'd had it when she returned to her room. Other than that, she had no idea when it had gone missing.

Afterward, he'd gone to the main floor and meandered through the crowds. Acting as if he were one of the hotel's guests, he switched between studying the movements of the employees and watching for any signs of their mysterious thief. So far he hadn't spotted anything out of the ordinary. No nervous body language, no one acting suspicious.

After an hour of wandering through the casino, he decided to head back to the bar and check in with Logan. Halfway there, his nostrils tingled with an offensive odor. One ingrained in his memory. One he hadn't scented in years.

He'd had plenty of reasons to remember the smell of a jackal, the ruthless scourge of the shifter world and enemy to all breeds. The first partner he'd had after becoming a cop had lost his life to one. His death had been bloody, the painful memory one Phelan tried to forget.

If he was scenting the distinct odor accurately, this one was male, possibly an alpha. What was the jackal doing in Phelan's pack's territory? And why was he just now picking up his scent? Phelan should have been able to detect him from the moment he'd entered the casino.

The more odor he inhaled, the harder his wolf pushed to transform. Phelan breathed through his mouth, minimizing the smell enough to keep his animal from shifting. Not wanting to waste any time, he retrieved his phone from his back pocket as he headed in the direction the scent was the strongest. He cursed when the call to Logan went straight to voicemail. Increasing his pace, yet not quite running, he moved through the crowds without drawing attention.

Within minutes, Phelan reached the blackjack area and the source of the problem. A large man with dark hair perched on the end of a chair mere feet away from Tessa. His black eyes were no longer human, and he clutched the table with claws extended. He wore the murderous glare of a male on the verge of completing a transformation.

All Phelan could see of Tessa was her back. He didn't need to see her face to sense what she was feeling. There was a rigid set to her shoulders, and her hands trembled at her sides. Taking a deep sniff, he picked up her fear laced with a mixture of irritation. It surrounded him, pulsed through him, and enraged the heck out of his wolf.

Rage ripped through him, along with the overwhelming need to protect her. His wolf raised his hackles, ready to rip the other man's throat out and forced his claws to extend from his fingertips. Phelan fisted his hands, forcing his nails into his palms, and fought to stay in control.

The humans at the nearby tables seemed unaware of what was transpiring. He caught the scent of at least four shifters—three wolves and a cougar. Glancing around, he easily picked the males out of the crowd. They remained nonthreatening though their stances were alert and wary.

Using the stealth of his wolf, Phelan kept his movements slow. He acknowledged each male in turn and signaled them to stay where they were. The last thing he needed was for anyone to transform and for things to get bloody.

#

Two things became obvious to Tessa at the same time. She had screwed up by saying Nira's name in front of Draven and now had confirmation that what Nira had told her was true.

Draven's fury pulsed across Tessa's skin, the air surrounding them filled with a thick cloud of tension. There was a feral gleam in his dark eyes, and she knew it was only a matter of time before he shifted. She didn't think he cared whether or not the humans in the room learned about the existence of shifters or that someone might get hurt when he revealed his animal form.

In situations like this, when confronted by another shifter—one more predatory and lethal than herself—not being able to change into her wolf was a bad thing. Ears drawn back, teeth bared, and prepared to attack, her animal was annoyed that all she could do was watch instead of sprouting fur, fangs, and claws.

Tessa wasn't usually one to back down from a fight. She knew better than to appear challenging. Having enhanced senses and the ability to heal quickly didn't mean she'd survive an assault. Shifters, even when they were young, could be vicious. When she was twelve, she'd gotten too close to one of her relatives during a transformation. It was his first time, and he'd lost control of the shift. Luckily, the painful injuries Tessa sustained weren't serious.

Overriding her wolf's need to control, Tessa hoped by showing submission and putting some space between them that Draven might calm down before things got ugly. She'd spotted four shifters nearby and had no doubt that things were about to get nasty.

Keeping her trembling hands at her sides, she dropped her chin and lowered her gaze. Any fast movements or signs of running would only encourage the jackal to give chase. She slowly took a step back from the table and bumped into a hard, unmoving wall of muscle.

Strong hands gripped her arms at the same time a familiar and enticing scent of woodsy spice and sexy male teased her senses. She didn't need to turn around to know her back was pressed up against Phelan's chest. Being near him caused a weakening in her knees, and an instantaneous heat shot to her core. Tall, gorgeously ripped, and possessing full, kissable lips, the man had appeared in more than one of her sexual fantasies. Extremely frustrating fantasies that she'd entertained almost every day since Ryland had introduced them.

What is he doing here? He rarely came to the casino unless he was with her brother. She only saw him at the monthly pack meetings, and even then he did his best to keep his distance from her. She couldn't figure out what she'd done to receive such a negative reaction from him. Unless he'd somehow discovered her secret, something shared by only her closest family members.

Wolves that couldn't shift were considered weak. Being a hybrid with an empathetic gift made her even less desirable. It would explain why he avoided her and why she'd catch him frowning at her when he didn't think she was paying attention. A fact that still bothered her and, if she was being honest, hurt her feelings.

"Are you okay?" he whispered, his mouth close to her ear, his warm breath trailing across her skin.

"Fine." She tipped her head back and locked gazes with an intense pair of dark sienna eyes. Eyes that appeared more wolf than human. Having Phelan this close, actually touching her, sent delicious shivers along her skin. Her wolf, along with her traitorous body, wanted to press in closer. Wanted to rub all over him, bathe in his nearness and enjoy the feeling of safety he offered.

"What are you doing here?" If Tessa hadn't been concentrating on calming Draven, she would have sensed him long before he had a chance to get behind her.

"Later," he said and pushed her to the side, keeping a hand wrapped around her wrist, ensuring his large frame stayed between her and Draven.

Considering Phelan's past behavior, the possessive move surprised her. She tamped down the urge to read more into his actions than trying to protect his partner's sister. He might appear composed, but anger radiated off him in brutal waves and seeped through the fringes of her shield.

She could feel the strength of his wolf and was amazed to discover that his animal was a lot more dominant than he let others see. The level of self-control it took for him to restrain his wolf's drive to shift was impressive. He'd earned her respect, and she couldn't help being drawn to him a little more.

"Is there a problem?" Unlike her, Phelan glared directly at Draven, refusing to be intimidated.

A couple of people at a nearby table had taken notice of the confrontation. After a quick glance, Tessa noted that the four shifters she'd spotted earlier had taken positions where they could easily assist if it became necessary.

"No, no problem at all." Draven sniffed the air and must have come to the same conclusion. He rolled his shoulders, retracted his claws, and sat back in his chair.

"Glad to hear it." Phelan released her wrist and took a step closer to Draven. "Why don't you take a walk with me? I have someone who would like to meet you. He'd be interested in hearing about your plans to leave the city."

Anyone who overheard Phelan's words would assume he was being friendly. Tess didn't miss the underlying threat and neither did Draven. His gaze narrowed and red flushed across his cheeks. The tension between them simmered like a pot of stew on the verge of boiling.

Draven fingered the stone on the pendant and sneered. "Please let *Kern* know my business in Vegas is personal. I won't be leaving until it is finished." Disdain dripped from every word.

It was the second time Draven had mentioned her family, confirming her suspicion that he knew he was infringing on their territory the minute he'd entered the casino. Other than the claw marks on the table, Draven hadn't actually caused any problems. Technically, Phelan couldn't do anything to him, and Draven had to know he wouldn't force the issue, not with this many people around.

"I'm done here." Draven downed the remainder of his drink. After slamming the glass on the table, he slid from the chair. He pinned Tessa with a menacing glare. "See you again soon, *Tessa*." Phelan might not have understood what Draven meant, but it didn't stop him from growling or staring at him until he'd disappeared from sight.

Oh, hell. Draven's threat was clear and caused a shudder to slither down her spine. He didn't know she knew about his plans, but she did know about Nira, and that was enough to put her on his radar. She gulped in air and reached for the table, curling her fingers around the edge to steady her shaking hands.

Phelan nodded at the four men who'd shown their support. They each returned the gesture, their way of letting him know they'd be close by if he needed them, then faded into the crowd. Once they were gone, he focused his attention on her. "Tessa?"

Noting his frown was all it took to put her on a defensive edge. "What?"

"Do you want to tell me what that was all about?" He ran his hand roughly through his hair. "Why you had a jackal on the verge of attacking you?"

No. "His name is Draven Thorn, and he doesn't like to lose." It was a lame excuse but the only one she was willing to give him.

"Really." Feigning innocence wasn't getting past his scrutinizing stare. "I need to find Logan and let him know what's going on." He pulled out his cell phone and swiped the screen. After a few seconds, he tucked the phone back in his pocket. "No answer. He was working the bar the last time I saw him." He placed a hand on her elbow. "Come with me. He'll want to hear what you know about our uninvited visitor."

That was all she needed, an interrogation where Logan played the good cop to Phelan's bad. Not going to happen. "I already told you I don't know anything." She hated not being truthful, but she didn't know him well enough to trust him. She pulled her arm free. "Besides, I still have work to do."

"Work can wait. I'd feel better if you came with me." He rubbed her lower back, the sensation meant to relax her, to persuade her. It almost worked until she thought about Nira.

She glanced at Phelan and wondered how he'd react if she told him she was an empath and had telepathically linked minds with a fairy. Or that Nira was trapped in a pendant and Tessa was working on a plan to get it away from the jackal.

If she was struggling with the facts, how did she expect Phelan to believe her? He was too much like Ryland. The cop in him wouldn't believe her unless she provided him with proof. Thinking about proof reminded her that she needed to find Draven.

Unfounded or not, Tessa believed Nira was telling the truth. She needed to do something; otherwise, people she cared about were going to get hurt—or worse. Knowing how overprotective her family was, she couldn't tell them what she knew until she had the pendant. Logan would order her to stay put. He'd lock her away in one of the hotel rooms and tell her it was for own safety.

Ryland would agree and tell her to let him handle it, and the rest of the family would back them up. By the time she got done arguing with them, Draven would be gone and it would be too late.

No, she'd have to handle this part herself. What was that old saying? Something about asking for forgiveness later rather than getting permission. She didn't have time for explanations and neither did Nira.

First, she had to get away from Phelan. She decided to use a well-tested note from Aurelia's handbook on how to get out of work. Tessa pressed her hand to her stomach and leaned heavily against the table.

"Are you okay?" He caressed her arm, his warm hand lingering near her elbow. "Do you need to sit down?"

"I'm feeling a little light-headed. I probably shouldn't have skipped lunch." She pushed away the guilt, reminding herself she was doing this for a good cause.

"What can I do to help?"

"Nothing." She shook her head. "Why don't you go find Logan? I'll grab something to eat and wait for you in the employee break room."

"I don't think I should leave you alone," Phelan said.

"I'll be fine. Whoever is on break can keep me company until you get there." *The lies are stacking up.* They were shorthanded, and Tessa knew there wouldn't be anyone to wait with her.

He appeared to waver on his decision, then finally said, "Okay, but you stay there until we come for you."

"I promise." Tessa patted his arm and gave him what she hoped was an innocent smile, then walked away before he could change his mind. She kept her strides slow and even, tamping down the urge to bolt as she maneuvered through the crowd.

When she reached the door restricted for employee use only, she glanced over her shoulder. Phelan was watching her, his gaze wary and combined with something she didn't recognize. At least he wasn't frowning, which she thought was a plus.

Once the door closed behind her, she bypassed the break room and headed down the long hallway leading to the women's locker room. She didn't have time to change, so she grabbed the backpack with her additional clothes out of her locker and headed back toward the casino.

With any luck, Phelan had gone to search for Logan. He might be suspicious of her actions but Draven's presence was a potential threat. His loyalty belonged to the pack, and he'd seek out her uncle. Logan wouldn't waste any time coming to find her and ensure she was safe. He'd also put the rest of the family and pack members on alert, which meant she'd have to act quickly if she wanted to retrieve the pendant.

Pushing the door open a crack, she peeked into the casino. When she didn't see any sign of Phelan, she ducked between the nearest row of slot machines. Maneuvering along the aisles, she worked her way in the same direction she'd last seen Draven.

Tessa found a less crowded area near the bathrooms. She wasn't sure how telepathy worked and hoped if she lowered her mental shield, she'd be able to contact Nira. Even with a handful of people, the emotions that seeped into her mind were overwhelming. She focused on clearing her mind. *"Nira, can you hear me?"* Nothing. A few seconds later, she tried again and still nothing.

Now what am I supposed to do? Determined to find an area where there weren't any people, Tessa left the gaming area and headed for the hotel lobby. Luck finally decided to give her some help. She didn't need to talk to Nira, not when her wolf caught a strong whiff of Draven's scent. First, she'd find the jackal, then she'd worry about how she was going to get the pendant from around his neck.

CHAPTER FIVE

Draven's actions didn't make any sense. Tessa thought
for sure his scent would lead her outside the building.
Instead, she'd tracked him to the hotel's restaurant and
bar, the Royal Stag. The restaurant portion had stopped
serving meals about a half hour ago, but the bar was still
open. She remained outside the restaurant for fear Draven
might be able to scent her. The last thing she wanted was
for him to find out she was following him.

Tessa wished she knew how the mental mind
connection worked so she could link with Nira again. So
far the two attempts she'd made had been worthless.
Maybe she needed to be closer to the pendant or actually
touching it to reconnect. She tried to imagine how awful it
was for Nira to be trapped outside her body. After Nira's
troubling remarks, Tessa worried the younger woman
might be in even more trouble. She'd feel a lot better and
less stressed if she could talk to Nira again.

Leaning near the frame to avoid detection from inside,
she peered through the large plate glass window etched
with a magnificent male deer standing in a beautiful
wilderness setting. A young couple, immersed in a
conversation, were the only ones who occupied a table.

Tessa noted the small bouquet of white daisies mixed with baby's breath sitting next to the woman and guessed they were newlyweds.

From her position, she caught a side view of Draven casually perched on a cushion-lined stool near the far end of the bar. He had his hands wrapped around a tall glass and appeared to be flirting with Rita, the human working behind the bar.

Because of her friendly and amorous nature, many of the male customers were drawn to the gorgeous blonde. It didn't hurt that she wore a sleeveless, sheer navy-blue dress that exposed some of her long neck and cleavage. Cleavage she flashed at Draven when she leaned across the bar to set a clean napkin and fresh drink in front of him.

Draven had a lot of nerve remaining inside the Fox and Hound after his run-in with Phelan. His plan to steal Nira's essence either made him extremely arrogant or he had a specific reason for targeting her family. Whatever his plans were, she hoped she was successful in putting a stop to them.

A dreadful thought occurred to Tessa, and the stressful knot she'd had in her stomach since meeting Draven tightened. What if her pack weren't the only shifters he was going after? Vegas attracted several different breeds, and a number of the families had made the city their home.

Nira had warned her that he'd be unstoppable if he succeeded in harnessing her fairy powers. What better opportunity to take over a huge territory and destroy all his enemies at once?

If her assumption was correct, then she was in way over her head and needed help. The only member of the family who'd be remotely willing to believe her story and offer assistance, instead of locking her away, was Brayden. He was her adventurous, oftentimes rebellious, uncle and Logan's younger brother. He was also the Royal Stag's manager, and there a good chance he was still working.

Feeling less overwhelmed and slightly better about the situation, Tessa headed for the back entrance with access through the kitchen. She found Troy, one of her uncle's employees, loading a white plastic rack of plates into the dishwasher. "Hey, Tessa. How's it going?"

"Going good." *Not really.* Especially since she was tracking a jackal and trying to rescue a fairy. "How about you?"

"Busy night." He glanced at all the bins filled with dirty dishes and sighed. "Hopefully, I'll get out of here before midnight."

Over the years, Tessa had helped out in the restaurant more times than she could count. She knew for a fact Troy wasn't getting out of there anytime soon but wasn't going to mention it. "Is Brayden still around?"

"'Fraid he already left for the night and won't be back until tomorrow. Rita's closing. Is there anything she can help you with?"

"No. It wasn't anything important." *Damn it, that figures.* The one time she needed help was the one time it wouldn't be available. "I'll catch up with him later."

"All right. I better get back to work." He returned to the sink and grabbed the long hose hanging overhead, then sprayed off a dirty plate and placed it in another rack.

"Hey, Troy." Tessa heard Rita's voice seconds before the swinging doors leading out into the restaurant burst open.

She didn't want the other woman to see her, so she quickly ducked into the kitchen and crouched out of sight. Rita liked to visit, and she loved to gossip. Normally, Tessa wouldn't care, but tonight she didn't have time to waste, and she wasn't in the mood to answer a bunch of questions.

"Yeah, what's up?" He must have released his grip on the sprayer handle, because Tessa didn't hear the water running anymore.

"My last customer wants a private tour of the pool area, and I told him I'd be happy to show him around. If you know what I mean."

Since when did employees give private tours to guests? There was a hot tub near the pool area. The way the two had been flirting in the bar, Tessa had a good idea what Rita planned to do with Draven when they got there. She'd worry about dealing with Rita's disregard for company policy later.

"What else is new," Troy grumbled.

"Anyway…" Rita sounded irritated. "Can you lock up back here when you're done? I'll lock up the front on my way out."

"Yeah, sure. It's not like I have a life or anything."

"You're a dear. I promise I'll make it up to you." The clack of heels on the tiled floor, followed by a swishing noise, let Tessa know Rita had returned to the bar.

"Dishwasher…shit job…should quit." Troy's comments were drowned out by the sound of spraying water and glass clanking against glass.

Tessa felt bad for Troy. Any other time, she'd be tempted to stay and help him finish cleaning so he could get out of there. Unfortunately, she needed to go.

Rita had no idea Draven was a shifter, much less a deadly and lethal one. After the way he'd acted in the casino, Tessa was worried he might do something to her when he got her alone.

The pool and spa were closed and locked for the evening. Most of the managers and some of the staff, including Tessa, had a set of keys. Rita was Brayden's assistant, so she wouldn't have any problems gaining access. Tessa knew a shortcut and planned to get there ahead of them.

Tessa loved to swim, but sometimes, like now, the smell of chlorine irritated her nostrils. At least it would help hide her scent. She'd arrived in the hot tub area minutes before Rita and Draven, then ducked into one of the small changing rooms. She didn't know how long she'd been sitting on the tiny bench with her knees tucked tightly against her chest. Her rear was going to sleep, and her clothes clung uncomfortably to her skin from all the steam.

If she had to listen to Rita giggle at one more of Draven's sexual innuendos, she was going to scream. Finally, after what seemed like forever, it sounded like they'd entered the tub's warm, bubbling water.

It didn't take long before she heard Rita moaning and decided it was safe to leave her hiding place. Too afraid that opening the door would alert Draven to her presence, she crawled through the gap near the floor.

Eww, just eww. Tessa made the mistake of glancing toward the hot tub, seeing their tangled and naked bodies, and wished she hadn't. After tonight, she would probably start drinking. Heavily. Though she didn't believe any amount of liquor was going to erase the image of what those two were doing in the water.

She spotted their clothes tossed carelessly on one of the white lounge chairs. To her relief, he'd taken off the pendant and hung it on the back of the chair. The way he'd gripped it earlier, Tessa had been surprised he'd remove it from around his neck.

She crawled toward the lounger on her hands and knees, constantly glancing over her shoulder to make sure she hadn't been seen. Her hand was inches from the pendant when she heard Rita's raspy voice, "Tessa, is that you?"

"Um." Tessa's pulse raced and notched even higher when she heard Draven growl. She didn't require further motivation to get to her feet and grab the pendant. She ignored the "no running" rule posted in bright red letters on the nearby wall and dashed for the security exit.

Everything was going great. She was feet from reaching her destination. Too bad she hadn't seen that damn puddle of water. Her foot slipped, and she lurched sideways. No matter how much she flailed her arms, she couldn't keep from falling. Couldn't keep the side of her rib cage from colliding with the metal frame of another lounge chair.

The shock rolling across Rita's features was nothing compared to the ferocious look Draven was giving her. Tessa tried not to stare at his male part swinging in the wind as he climbed out of the pool and started toward her. She was more focused on the change to his pupils and the sharp claws extending from his fingertips.

She caught a glimpse of Rita grabbing her clothes and heading for the security gate leading to the pool area on the opposite side of the room. Tessa stopped worrying about her safety.

"*Tessa*," he snarled, sounding more animal than human. "Give me the pendant."

Scrambling to her feet, she shoved the chair in his path and bolted toward the exit.

Draven managed to jump over the chair. Lucky for Tessa, the water dripping from his feet caused him to slip and stumble, slowing his attempt to close the distance. He landed on his hands and knees, then glared at her. "You bitch. I'm going to kill you when I catch you."

She had no doubt he meant it and lunged for the locked door. Her hand shook so bad, it took her several tries to get the key card out of her pocket. She made the mistake of glancing over her shoulder as she slid the card over the access panel. Draven's outstretched hand, claws poised to strike, was within a foot of reaching her. She squealed and wrenched the handle, spinning around to shut the door behind her. The lock clicking into place was the best noise she'd heard all day.

She heard a thud and assumed Draven had slammed into the door. Loud cursing, banging, and more growling followed. Tessa didn't think he could get through the door, but she wasn't going to stick around and test the theory. Now that she had the pendant, she needed to find a safe place to hide it. She also needed to figure out what to do next and how to keep Draven from following through on his death threat.

#

Phelan had remained in the gaming area for several minutes after he watched Tessa disappear behind the employee-restricted access door. He was unable to shake the unsettling feeling he had about Draven's parting and couldn't stop wondering what had happened between her and the jackal.

There was no dismissing the amount of rage Draven had displayed, or the wild, almost savage glint in his eyes. Something besides losing a few games of blackjack had set him off, pushed him to the edge of a complete shift.

He'd bet all his years of experience as a cop that Tessa knew the answer. She'd appeared shaken and scared. There was a moment when he'd held her gaze and thought she might tell him what had happened. He wasn't sure why, but something had changed her mind.

Instinct, and his irate wolf, warned him not to let her leave, to follow her and keep her safe. As far as his animal was concerned, Tessa belonged to him, to them. Phelan had never been possessive or protective of a female before and hadn't wanted to leave her either. He had every intention of acting on his instinct, but first he needed to find Logan and warn him about Draven.

He'd contemplated the notion of tossing her over his shoulder and taking her with him. He didn't think Logan would appreciate him manhandling his niece, and from the stories Ryland had shared about their childhood adventures, he knew Tessa would have put up one heck of a fight.

It took every ounce of Phelan's self-control to walk

away and head for the bar at the other end of the casino. He'd questioned a couple of the employees, including the brunette waitress he'd seen earlier. None of them had seen Logan in the last thirty minutes or had any idea where he'd gone. Frustrated, Phelan tried calling again. When he didn't get a response, he sent a text telling Logan he needed to speak with him urgently.

Phelan was on his way back to Tessa when his phone rang. He slipped it out of his pocket and released a relieved sigh when he saw Logan's name.

"You needed me?" Logan spoke in an abrupt tone, an indication that Phelan must have interrupted something important. "Don't tell me you found the person this quickly."

"No, we have a bigger problem."

"What kind of problem?" He imagined Logan grinding his teeth and pinching the bridge of his nose.

"Nothing I can discuss on the phone. Can you meet me in the employee break room?" Phelan had left Tessa alone a lot longer than he'd planned. The need to see her, to touch her, weighed more heavily on him with each passing minute.

Logan wasn't alone. Phelan could hear another man's voice in the background. He couldn't understand what he was saying. "Forget the break room."

Phelan was about to argue, but Logan cut him off with his next command. "I need you in the security room." The line went dead, and Phelan stared at his phone.

Now what?

Five minutes later, Phelan walked into the hotel's impressive surveillance room. The Kerns must have spent a fortune on the state-of-the-art equipment they used to surveil and protect their property. Two of the four walls were lined with viewing monitors covering everything from the casino to the outside parking lot. A long rectangular table containing computers, keyboards, and a telephone was positioned in the middle of the room parallel to the screens.

"Zach." Phelan directed his greeting to the man sitting at the far end of the table tapping keys and manually changing the views on the screens. He'd met Ryland's younger cousin and the security supervisor on several other occasions.

"Hey, Phelan." Zach gave him a brief nod, then returned his attention to the monitor in front of him.

"What's going on?" Phelan glanced at Logan, who was standing to his right, arms crossed, and lips pressed together in a tense line.

"Before we discuss your problem, I want you to see something." Logan pointed to one of the screens. "Zach, replay it again."

Phelan stared at the screen, wondering what had the man so upset. A few seconds later, Tessa appeared in the footage, and he groaned. What was she doing in the hot tub area when she'd promised him she'd wait in the break room?

He continued to watch as she grabbed what appeared to be a necklace or pendant off the back of a lounge chair. On screen, Tessa rushed across the room, the chain dangling from her fisted hand. He thought his heart was going to explode when Draven appeared on the screen, naked and angry. He barely noticed the woman in the background grabbing her clothes. His focus was on the jackal and his attempt to get to Tessa.

Phelan's wolf snarled and snapped, ready to go for Draven's throat. The jackal had threatened his female and needed to die. Phelan, the man, was in total agreement. Rage remained with him long after he saw Tessa escape safely through the security door.

Intent on getting to Tessa, Phelan had taken only two steps when Logan grabbed his arm. "Wait. Where are you going?"

"To find Tessa." Phelan hadn't realized he'd growled

until Logan quirked a brow and released his arm.

"I have people searching the hotel for her and the man on the footage. They'll let us know as soon as they find either of them. Do you know who the man is?" Logan asked.

Phelan clenched his fists, fighting to remain calm. "All I know is he's a jackal, and Tessa said his name was Draven Thorn." The nearest jackal pack was located in Arizona, and there was a chance Logan had crossed paths with Draven or had possibly heard his name. "Do you know why he's here?"

"No idea, but you can be damned sure I'm going to find out. I'll have Ryland do some checking and see if he can find any information on him." Logan crossed his arms and continued staring at Draven's frozen image on the screen. "When did you speak to my niece, and how exactly does she know him?" There was that overprotective tone Phelan had come to expect from the Kern males whenever Tessa's name was mentioned in a conversation.

Shrugging the tension from his shoulders, Phelan spent the next few minutes telling him about the jackal and their confrontation. As he'd expected, Logan was pissed when he learned a jackal had threatened Tessa. Not that he blamed him. Phelan was still struggling with similar emotions. Feeling helpless as he'd watched the video of Tessa being attacked by Draven had only made the situation worse.

Zach, who'd remained silent until now, pointed out the obvious. "I hate to even suggest it because I think the world of Tessa. Do you think she's the one stealing from the customers?"

"I refuse to believe she had anything to do with the thefts." Logan ran his hand roughly through his hair. "This has to be something else."

"Any idea what it could be?" Phelan didn't know Tessa all that well, but from their brief encounters, he'd learned she was independent, smart, and caring. He honestly didn't believe she was capable of stealing from her family. He agreed with Logan. After the frightened way she'd reacted to Draven at the blackjack table, there had to be another reason why she'd taken the pendant from him.

"No clue." Logan shifted his gaze to Phelan. "Did she say anything to you earlier? Anything that would indicate what happened between them or what she was planning to do?"

"She gave me some excuse about him being upset when he lost. I got the impression she knew more than she was letting on." Phelan doubted it would have done any good, and he regretted not pushing her harder for the information.

"And the last time you saw her?" Logan asked.

"She said she needed to eat and would wait for us in the break room." Guilt pinged in Phelan's chest. If he hadn't left her alone, none of this would have happened.

"Obviously, she never made it." Logan glanced at Zach, concern flickering across his features. "Did you check all the footage?"

Zach frowned and tapped some keys, changing the views on several of the screens. "Twice. The hallway outside the pool area is the last place she shows up anywhere. I also tried tracking her cell like you asked but got nothing. She must have turned it off."

Logan growled. "And Draven, were you able to track his movements?"

"I show him leaving the hotel alone through the front entrance not long after Tessa disappeared."

"Judging by the way he reacted, Draven is not going to stop searching for Tessa until he gets back what she took." Phelan had a feeling she'd get hurt or killed in the process.

"We need to find her before Draven does." Logan turned his attention back to Phelan. "Ryland told me you're the best damned tracker he's ever worked with, and I need a favor."

"Name it," Phelan said.

"I want you to find Tessa and bring her back safely. I'd do it myself, but I need to stay here and ensure measures are taken to alert and protect the rest of the pack."

"Don't worry. I'll find her." *Then I'll bend her over my knee and spank her fine backside for lying to me.* Phelan had already planned to go after her. Having the order come from his alpha ensured that anything he did to protect her would be supported.

"We need to keep this quiet until we figure out what the jackal is up to and why he's here. The last thing we need is to start a panic with the other families." Logan pinched the bridge of his nose. "I'll contact Brock and let him know what's going on. He might be able to help locate Draven."

"If there's anything else I can do to help…"

"Not right now. Your priority needs to be Tessa." Logan turned a scrutinizing glare toward Zach. "I'm guessing this isn't the first time Rita has taken a customer to the pool area after hours."

Zach swallowed nervously. "No idea. That's a new camera. The old one covered the main pool area. I had this one installed after the problems with the thefts started. The old one didn't cover the hot tub area."

"Great job." Logan nodded his approval. "Contact Rita and Brayden. I want them both in my office within the hour."

That was one meeting Phelan was glad he'd miss. He assumed Rita was the woman he'd seen grabbing her clothes. No doubt by the time Logan finished with the woman, she'd be in tears and without a job.

Phelan left the room intent on finding Tessa. She had to know messing with a jackal was dangerous. What was so important about the pendant that she was willing to risk her life to take it? He was determined to get answers to the question and a few others as soon as he found her. And he would find her, because nothing else was acceptable, to him or his wolf.

CHAPTER SIX

I am going to die. Images of Draven when he'd chased after Tessa played through her mind like a bad scene from a black-and-white horror flick. She dropped her head and braced her hands against the shower's pale-blue ceramic tiles. The warm water pelting against her neck and shoulders did nothing to alleviate her stress or the shudders she was still experiencing from her momentary lapse in sanity.

Tessa would love to blame her current predicament on Aurelia for not showing up for work, but she couldn't. The fault lay entirely with her, and she knew it. She'd been the one stupid enough to think she could take the pendant and save Nira by herself.

Why couldn't she be like the rest of the members in her family? Why did she have to be an empath? If Nira hadn't been able to access her mind, hadn't sounded so desperate, she'd probably be at home right now, asleep in her bed.

Her plan had been so simple, so easy. Grab the pendant without being seen. Find Nira. Stop Draven. Yet somehow she'd managed to screw it up. Draven had seen her. He knew her name and where she worked—at least for today. She couldn't guarantee she'd have a job once

Logan found out what she'd done. At the rate she was going, she might not live long enough to hear him yell at her.

Tessa groaned and leaned her forehead against the smooth, cool surface. It was only a matter of time before Draven tracked her down. When that happened, he'd rip out her throat, take the pendant, and finish the spell to bind Nira to him forever.

She was smart, tough, and needed to get a grip. This wasn't the first time she'd been confronted with feelings of inadequacy and found the strength to overcome them. If she could deal with her mother constantly pointing out her imperfections, along with her inability to shift, then she could deal with this.

She'd sensed how powerful Draven was when he'd partially shifted. He was an alpha, and they never traveled without an escort. He might have been by himself in the casino, but it didn't mean he'd come to the city alone. What if he had other pack members searching for her right now?

It was obvious by his actions that Draven didn't respect the laws of their kind. It was the reason she'd decided to leave the hotel. She hoped he'd be more interested in finding her and the pendant, which meant her family and their human guests would be safe.

As much as Tessa wished she could go home and curl up in her warm bed, it wasn't safe. Even if she hadn't learned a lot from having an older brother as a cop, she knew her small yet comfortable house would be the first place Draven would search for her.

Even sleeping on the lumpy couch at Aurelia's, listening to her scream her idiot boyfriend's name during sex, would have been preferable to the room she'd found at the Lucky Shamrock.

She remembered the cockroach-infested dive all too well from the one time she'd been here. It was within walking distance of her family's hotel and three blocks from the strip. At the time, her car had been in the shop, and she'd gotten a ride home from her cousin. Of course, her worthless boyfriend didn't have a vehicle of his own, so they had to pick him up from work on the way. Surprisingly, he'd lasted in the night clerk position for almost two weeks before getting fired.

Getting out of the Fox and Hound without being seen by security had been easy. Being family had its perks. Tessa knew where all the cameras were located from hanging out with her cousin Zach. She remembered to turn off her phone so Ryland wouldn't be able to use the Divisions' superior computer system to track her.

She'd even doused herself in the vanilla spray they kept in a basket on the counter of the women's bathroom for customer use to mask her scent. She didn't carry around a lot of cash, but she'd had enough to pay for the room, so a credit card purchase couldn't be traced.

By now, Phelan knew she'd lied to him. She wasn't worried about Logan finding out what had happened with Draven. Rita wouldn't say anything; she'd be too afraid she'd lose her job. Later, after she'd had a couple of hours to sleep, Tessa would call Logan and tell him what she'd done and where he could find her.

Reaching behind her, she twisted the stainless steel knobs and shut off the water. The towel she grabbed had seen better days, the fabric worn thin in several places. She had one foot out of the tub when she heard a loud bang, and froze.

Someone's in my room. She heard the sound of a toilet flushing through the poorly insulated wall. A nervous laugh escaped from her lips. Shaking her head, she chastised herself for being so jumpy and stepped the rest of the way out of the enclosure.

After she finished drying herself off, she slipped on her panties and tugged a T-shirt over her head. She grabbed another towel off the metal rack next to the sink and used it to get the excess moisture out of her long hair.

Her stomach rumbled, reminding her the hamburger and fries she'd had for lunch were long gone. She'd passed on the poor selection of outdated potato chips and candy bars in the hotel's vending machine when she'd arrived. She might have been able to find a sandwich or at least a hot dog at the convenience store down the block, but she'd been too afraid to wander around in public.

Opening the bathroom door, she came face-to-face with a man's chest. "What the he…" The stench of jackal prickling her nose made her forget whatever she was going to say. Glancing upward, she locked gazes with an intense pair of dark eyes. A jackal in her room couldn't be a coincidence, and she hated that she'd guessed right about Draven not traveling alone. How had they found her so quickly? She was certain she'd done a good job covering her trail.

"Hello, beautiful." His narrow lips widened into a wicked sneer. "Draven sends his regards."

Tessa screamed and spun around. She'd barely made it two steps into the bathroom before he clamped his hand over her mouth. He wrapped his strong, muscular arm around her waist, pinning her tightly to his chest and lifting her off the ground.

She grabbed at his arm and kicked his shins with her heels in an attempt to break free. Her wolf growled, scratched, and snarled right along with her. The actions were a waste of time. The man was a solid wall of muscle. "Where do you think you're going?" He chuckled and dragged her back into the bedroom.

He pressed his mouth near her ear. His hot breath fanned her neck, sending a dreadful chill skittering across her skin. "Stop struggling." He slid the hand on her mouth to her throat and squeezed.

A haze of black filled her periphery. The last thing she wanted was to lose consciousness. As soon as she stopped fighting, the grip around her throat lessened. She coughed and gulped in air.

"There's nothing here." Another man she hadn't noticed before moved to the old dresser pressed against the opposite wall. He yanked out the remaining drawer, then slammed it back in place. Other than the jagged scar along his jaw, he was a twin, an identical duplicate of the man standing behind her. He had the same overly bleached, spiked hair, black T-shirt, and matching leather jacket. Even the thick muscles of their broad chests appeared to be cloned from the same mold.

The man across from her reached into the front pocket of his jeans and pulled out a silver-and-black object. He pressed a tiny button along the edge, and a thin blade popped out. "I say we take care of her now and get out of here before someone calls the cops." He grinned and tapped the flat edge of the blade against his palm.

Tessa gasped and widened her eyes.

"Nah, Gregor. I think she's going to be a good girl and tell us where she hid the pendant, aren't you?"

No, I'm really not. "What pendant?" She wasn't stupid. They'd kill her as soon as she told them where it was hidden, which was in the bottom of her backpack and out of sight behind the bathroom door.

"Don't play games, bitch. I'm not as patient as my brother. We know you have it." Gregor took a menacing step closer. "Now where did you hide it?"

"You better tell him." The guy restraining her rubbed his knuckles against her cheek. "I'd sure hate to see this pretty face all cut up."

Tessa jerked her head away from his hand. "I have no idea what you're talking about." She tried to sound convincing and hide the fear racing through every one of her nerve endings.

"Screw cutting her up." Gregor folded the blade and tucked it back in his pocket. "I have a better idea." He reached inside his jacket and pulled out a syringe containing a glowing green liquid.

This can't be good. She had a feeling whatever was in that needle would be far worse than dealing with the knife. Unless the stabs were deep or they hit major organs, she could survive most cuts from a blade.

"Kynan, pin her down on the bed and hold her arm."

"Sorry sweetheart. You should have told us what we needed to know." Kynan lifted her off the ground and tossed her on her back.

Tessa screamed and tried to roll away, but Kynan moved too fast. In seconds, he had his hand clamped over her mouth again and had pressed his knee into her abdomen to keep her pinned to the mattress.

Gregor sneered admiringly at the syringe and removed the cap. "This here is a special concoction we got from a powerful witch. It's gonna make you tell us everything we want to know." He caressed the length of her arm with the backs of his fingers. "Too bad you aren't going to look very nice once this stuff gets done frying you from the inside out."

Tessa's pulse raced, and her chest tightened. Her muted screams and fruitless struggles brought tears to her eyes. She couldn't move, could barely breathe, could only stare at the long, sharp needle Gregor held inches from her arm.

Her wolf whimpered, riding close to the surface, frantically pushing for a shift that would never come.

#

Zach had informed Phelan that Tessa's car was still in the hotel parking lot. According to Logan, she lived too far away to travel on foot. His gut told him her home would be the last place she'd go. It would be the first place everyone would think to start, including Draven.

No, he didn't think she'd gone far. It wouldn't matter if Tessa had cleverly avoided being caught on any of the security cameras. When Phelan caught a scent, he could track anything, especially in his wolf form. Earlier, when he'd held her close, he'd gotten a whiff of her unique smell and had immediately imprinted it to memory. It was an enticing blend of honey, coconut, and sexy she-wolf.

After picking up her trail near the security door to the pool area, he quickly followed it to the women's restroom in the hotel lobby. He opened the door and had to step aside to make room for two older women he guessed to be in their late fifties to exit. He ignored their disgusted sneers and mutterings about him not being smart enough to find the men's bathroom.

Once inside, an overwhelming aroma of vanilla accosted his nostrils and irritated his senses. Why females would purposely douse themselves in the nauseatingly sweet smell was beyond him. Or so he thought until he picked up a hint of Tessa's faint scent near the complimentary basket and on the half-used bottle of body spray.

She must have realized Draven would come after her and done her best to mask her natural scent. The more he tracked her, the more he learned about her, the more impressed he became.

Any other time, he'd appreciate her ingenious tactics, but right now, he wanted to throttle her. Disguising her scent would definitely slow Draven down. Unfortunately, it also hindered Phelan's tracking ability. His wolf, upset that it was taking so long to find her, was getting more agitated and making things worse.

Phelan had one advantage he was certain the jackal didn't possess. During the mediocre assignments Brock had given him, he'd gained a few valuable contacts. Contacts he never would have gotten otherwise. If his boss hadn't been such a constant pain in his ass, Phelan might have taken the time to thank him. Then again, probably not.

Reaching into his back pocket, he retrieved his phone and selected a number. A few seconds later, a familiar male voice answered, "Glitter & Gold."

"Saul, it's Phelan."

"Phelan, my boy, long time. How have you been?"

"Fine…" Even though Saul had moved his family to Vegas and opened the pawn shop over ten years ago, Phelan could still detect hints of the East Coast accent in some of his words. To hear the old man tell it, the fox shifters were the most cunning breed in New York City.

Besides being the best pickpockets on the street, for the simple price of a cheap wristwatch, they could find anything or anyone. Foxes had a thing about watches, go figure.

They didn't much care for anyone who worked in the division, but like all other shifter breeds, they despised jackals more. He'd met Saul during one of his earlier assignments when Brock had him working the street. It had been one of those right place, right time kind of scenarios.

He'd walked out of the coffee shop next door to Saul's business and saw a man lift the back of his T-shirt and retrieve a gun tucked in the back of his pants. Phelan followed him into the pawn shop and was able to disarm him before he shot Saul's grandson. From that moment forward, he'd earned the respect of the entire Lewis family, which he'd learned later was considerable.

"But this ain't a social call, is it?"

"I'm afraid not." Phelan rubbed the back of his neck. He hated asking for favors or having to owe someone.

"You know I'll do anything I can for you, so get to the point, boy. I ain't got all day."

Phelan almost chuckled at the remark. Saul had a thriving business, but it wasn't like he had customers lined up on the street to get inside. More than likely the old guy was perched on the stool he kept behind the counter, drinking coffee and watching sports on one of any number of the HD flat screens he had on display around the shop. "I'm searching for someone and don't have a lot of time to find her." The threat to Tessa's life was real, and to say he had any time at all was an understatement.

"What's the gal's name you're so hot to find?"

Hot? Hot was putting it mildly, and it had nothing to do with Saul's insinuation that his search for Tessa might be of a sexual nature. He was ready to turn the city upside down to find her, and not because he was following an order from his alpha. Besides the primal protectiveness of his wolf, he was battling an overwhelming possessiveness to make the gorgeous shifter his own.

It didn't make any sense. It wasn't uncommon to be attracted to another shifter. Their animals were very sexual by nature. But this was different. He'd never heard of the deep primal urges surfacing unless someone had found their mate. Surely he'd know if Tessa was his mate, wouldn't he? His wolf was already convinced and was pushing him to find her. "Her name is Tessa Shaw."

Phelan heard what sounded like spitting, then choking, and imagined Saul had been in the middle of drinking something.

"Are you talking about Logan Kern's niece? *That* Tessa?"

"Yeah, do you know her?" Phelan wasn't surprised he knew Logan. As big as Vegas was, it was a small world when it came to the shifters. Why did the sound of Saul's voice suddenly make him uneasy? The man knew a lot about what happened on the streets. Was he already too late to save her?

"I know her all right. She's special, like family." There was a brief pause before Saul started speaking again. "I like you, Phelan, really do. But if you've done anything to hurt that sweet gal, I'll…"

Hurt her. No. Find her, possess her, keep her safe. Yes. "She's in trouble. There's a jackal by the name of Draven Thorn after her. Ever heard of him?"

"No. And what is a jackal doing in wolf territory, and why is he after Tessa?" Phelan could hear the anger in Saul's tone and imagined a frown creasing his thick brows.

"I don't know the why, but I do know she'll end up

dead if I don't find her first." Someday, when Phelan had the time, he would ask Saul how he knew Tessa and why he thought the world of her.

"Where'd you see her last?" Saul asked.

"At her family's hotel."

"I have a nephew who works the area near there. Let me contact him, see what he knows. Stay close to your phone." Saul disconnected the call. Some family traits were hard to break. Working the area probably meant his nephew was either a pickpocket or involved in a similar form of making money. Phelan wasn't going to ask, nor was he going to investigate. Not if the less than legal source helped him find Tessa.

It only took five minutes before he received a call back from Saul. "My sources think they saw her heading into the office over at the Lucky Shamrock."

"What's that?" It sounded like the name of a casino. Since Phelan was still learning his way around the city, he figured the name could apply to anything.

"Sleazy hotel three blocks east of the strip. I'll text you the address."

"Thanks, I owe you."

"You don't owe me nothing, never will. My grandson is alive because of you." There was a pause on the other end of the line. "Phelan."

"Yeah."

"You keep her safe, and call if you need any help."

"I will." Phelan disconnected the call and waited for the information, hoping he wasn't already too late.

CHAPTER SEVEN

Phelan parked his truck in the trash-littered parking lot of the Lucky Shamrock. Saul hadn't been kidding when he'd mentioned the run-down condition of the property. There were numerous holes in the hotel's neon sign, and some of the letters had burned out. A considerable amount of the two-story building's white exterior paint was worn and peeling.

Patches of dirt that might once have contained flowers were overgrown with weeds. The faded orange door leading to one of the first-floor rooms had a large crack running down the center as if someone had tried to kick their way through it.

The early morning temperatures had already reached the lower eighties and promised another hot and humid day. Intent on getting the number to the room where Tessa might be staying, he entered the small office located on the far corner of the L-shaped building.

A young man who appeared to be in his early twenties was perched on a stool behind the reservation counter. Phelan didn't think the air-conditioning was working, because it was considerably hotter in the small room than it was outside. The rotating fan sitting on the desk behind him wasn't doing much more than pushing the air around.

The clerk had his elbows propped on the counter, head clasped between his hands. He appeared to be too engrossed in the magazine spread out in front of him to notice Phelan. After clearing his throat and getting no response, Phelan pulled out his badge and waved it in front of the guy's face.

Raising his head, he used both hands to tuck his dark, stringy hair behind his ears. "What do ya want, Officer?" He enunciated each syllable of the last word. He appeared emotionless, as if visits from law enforcement were a daily occurrence.

"I need to know if a woman by the name of Tessa Shaw got a room within the last few hours?"

He scratched his chin, stared at the ceiling speculatively, then answered, "Nope."

"She may have used another name. Tall, long dark hair, and gray eyes."

"You mean the hot babe wearing the short skirt. Nice set of legs and a mighty fine ass."

Phelan wasn't thrilled about his comment. He fisted his hands to keep from yanking the kid across the counter and teaching him some manners. His wolf released a warning growl, unhappy that another male had ogled what clearly belonged to him. "What room?"

"Room 220." The kid shrugged. "Same thing I told the other guys." He dropped his gaze back to the magazine.

"What. Other. Guys?" Tension rippled through Phelan, and he slapped his hand on the counter when he didn't get an answer right away.

The kid jumped, nearly falling off his stool. He held up his hands in a defensive manner. "I don't know, man. Two guys...white hair...mean-looking...could be twins. You just missed 'em."

The muscles in his chest clamped so tight, Phelan could hardly get air into his lungs. He'd expected to get a brief description of Draven, not hear there were others after

Tessa. What had she gotten herself into? Was he already too late to do anything about it?

"Where's the room?" he snarled.

"Back of the building, second floor."

Phelan shoved the door open and raced across the parking lot toward the staircase on the other end of the building. As soon as he reached the bottom of the staircase, he detected the lingering scent of jackal. Two distinct smells and both male. Taking the steps two at a time, Phelan quickly reached the exterior walkway for the upper landing. He kept moving, checking the number assignments on the doors until he found 220.

The door was closed, but the wood around the handle and lock were splintered as if someone had forced it open. He heard a male voice and a woman's muffled whimper coming from inside. Instead of using caution, he shoved the door hard, causing it to thwack loudly against the inside wall.

One of the bleached-blond lookalikes had Tessa pinned to the bed with his hand clamped over her mouth. The other one gripped her wrist and was about to plunge a needle attached to a syringe containing a glowing green liquid into her arm. They simultaneously jerked their heads in his direction, flaring their nostrils and baring their teeth.

"Who are you?" asked the man pressing Tessa into the bed.

"I'm the guy who's going to rip your throat out for touching her." Rage ripped through Phelan when Tessa's fear-filled gaze locked with his and he saw the tears streaming down the side of her face. "Let her go," he growled, allowing his wolf a partial shift to expose his fangs and claws. He lunged at the man holding the syringe, yanking him away from her. Their bodies slammed into the wall next to the bathroom. The force was strong enough to tear through the red-and-gold striped wallpaper and leave a large dent in the plaster.

The man roared and pushed Phelan away from him,

then braced his hand against the wall to get back on his feet. He gripped the syringe and wielded it like a weapon, aiming for any part of Phelan he could reach.

Phelan dodged the man's movements. He kept his focus on the sharp point, aware that the other man had dragged Tessa off the bed, one arm wrapped around her waist, the other encircling her throat.

"Gregor, what are you waiting for? Take care of him already," the man holding Tessa ordered.

As soon as Gregor swiped at him again, Phelan grabbed his wrist and slammed him into the wall. He banged Gregor's right arm against the solid surface. On the third attempt, Gregor finally released the syringe and it dropped to the floor.

Gregor growled and used his free hand to punch Phelan in the ribs. He winced, grabbed his side and stepped backward, but not far enough to keep Gregor from catching him in the jaw with a right hook. Phelan ignored the salty taste in his mouth and responded with a knee to Gregor's stomach, followed by a similar punch to his face. Gregor staggered to the side, doubled over, and landed on his knees.

"Phelan, watch out!" Tessa shouted.

He spun around and noticed that the other man had tossed her onto the bed and was moving toward him, claws extended. With Gregor on the floor near his feet, Phelan didn't have much room to maneuver. He took several steps backward, hoping to draw the man closer to the door and away from Tessa.

A woman's scream tore through the room. Phelan glanced over his shoulder and spotted an older woman with olive-toned skin and short black hair standing on the landing outside the hotel room. She wore a light pink uniform and had the fingers of one hand curled tightly around the bar of a small cart filled with towels and cleaning supplies.

Phelan quickly hid his fangs, retracted his claws, and

stepped back from the doorway. The woman's screaming became a monotonous shrill of Spanish. It wouldn't be long before she drew the attention of other hotel occupants. The man who was standing retracted his claws, reached down, and helped Gregor to his feet.

With the presence of too many humans and no backup, attempting to detain the two men would be impossible even if he were able to shift. Phelan's primary concern was protecting Tessa. Keeping his narrowed gaze on the two men, he moved closer to the bed. He held his hand out to Tessa, pulling her behind him the minute her feet landed on the floor.

The two men eased past Phelan and moved out of the room. Gregor snarled at the woman, causing her to gasp, release the cart, and back into the railing. The other man gritted his teeth and growled at Phelan. "Next time you won't be so lucky." He crammed the cart into the empty doorway, then disappeared after Gregor.

Phelan took a deep breath, tamping down the anger rifling through him, and turned around to face Tessa. If he'd arrived a minute later, she'd probably be dead. The thought left his emotions raw and unsettled. He was torn between throttling her and pulling her into his arms. Instead, he gently cupped her damp cheek. "Are you okay? Did they hurt you?"

"A little bruised, but I'm fine," she said in a raspy voice.

"I need you to stay here while I make sure they're gone." Phelan hated leaving her alone, but he couldn't take the chance that the jackals wouldn't come back, or that there weren't others close by. "Will you do that for me, please?" He didn't have time to press her for answers and didn't think she would take off again when she nodded.

Phelan maneuvered the cart out of the doorway and stepped out onto the landing. There was no sign of the twins. He glanced at the small group of people hovering close by and flashed his badge. "There's nothing to see here. Go back to your rooms."

He noticed a few disappointed expressions as the guests shuffled away. The cleaning woman rolled her eyes and made a humphing noise. She mumbled something in Spanish and pushed the cart in the opposite direction.

Phelan headed for the staircase, checking the area between the hotel and the adjacent building. Finding nothing of concern, he hurried to the lower level. When he reached the bottom of the stairs, he spotted one of the men in the passenger seat of a car moving rapidly through the parking lot. He managed to get a glimpse of the license plate number and made a mental note to call Ryland later and have him run it through the system.

After sending Logan a text letting him know Tessa was safe, he headed back to the room. He needed to get her to safety, then he planned to find out what she had gotten herself into.

#

Phelan's request not to leave might have sounded like a plea, but his gaze held the intensity of his wolf, reminding her that he meant business and wasn't taking no for an answer.

Tessa had no intention of going anywhere after what had happened. She might not be a genius, but she wasn't an idiot either. It was obvious her attempts to cover her tracks had been a complete failure. Not only had her plan to save Nira gone to shit, it had nearly gotten her killed. Her blood still pulsed through her veins faster than a race car doing laps.

Too shaken to reach the bed, she leaned against the wall, giving in to her weakened knees, and slid to the floor. She wrapped her arms around her chest and gulped in air, trying to calm down and figure out what she was going to do next.

She should have known Draven would send someone

after her. Destructive and dangerous alphas, men obsessed with the need to control, never acted alone. They always had others, betas who were drawn to their higher level of power and more than willing to do their bidding. The shifter world was no different from the human world in that respect. All leaders needed followers to even things out.

Tessa couldn't believe she was alive. Memories of how close that needle had come to being shoved into her vein made her shiver. Rubbing her arms, she tried to push away the reminder that she would have suffered an excruciating death if Phelan hadn't miraculously arrived when he did.

More than a little grateful, she felt guilty for lying to him earlier. She knew he'd be angry when he didn't find her in the break room. She figured he might search for her, but she never believed he'd actually find her. Not here.

Thinking about Phelan and how he'd found her, how he rescued her, didn't provide any answers, it only created more questions. Why was he the one searching for her? If anything, she expected someone from her family, most likely Logan, to find her. Had Phelan somehow discovered she'd taken the pendant? Did he think she was a thief, and planned to whisk her off to jail? She still didn't think he'd believe her story, and if he locked her up, there'd be no one to help Nira.

Phelan hadn't shut the door before he left, and movement near the doorway drew Tessa from her thoughts. From where she was sitting, she couldn't tell who was out there. It was probably another guest hoping to get a glimpse inside and see what had happened during Phelan's fight with the jackals. Not in the mood to deal with any additional attention, she pushed up from the floor. She straightened her bunched-up T-shirt and tugged it to the tops of her thighs.

A middle-aged man wearing nothing more than a pair of dark sweats leaned against the black wrought iron railing. A grin slowly spread along his lips as he leered at her and scratched his crotch. "Err," she groaned, ready to tell the disgusting pervert if he didn't stop staring, she'd rip off his balls. With her luck, he'd probably enjoy it. She shook her head and slammed the door in his face, annoyed that he had the nerve to chuckle.

Between Phelan and the jackals destroying the lock and dead bolt, no amount of coaxing would keep the darned thing shut. She couldn't even secure the door with the chain. There was a hole in the plaster near the frame, and the slide plate dangled from the lock mounted on the door.

Blowing out an exasperated sigh, she grabbed the only chair in the room, tilted it so it rested on the back legs, then wedged it underneath the door handle.

Knowing Phelan would return soon, she headed for the bathroom to finish dressing. After what happened, he'd no doubt be in what she liked to call "the cop interrogation mode." The same label she applied to Ryland whenever he played the role of overbearing brother, had questions, and wanted answers she wasn't willing to give.

On her way to the bathroom, Tessa retrieved the syringe from the floor. She didn't want anyone to find it and do something stupid with it. Glancing around, she found the plastic cap and sealed it over the tip of the needle. She retrieved her backpack from behind the door and slipped the syringe into one of the side pockets.

After reassuring herself that the pendant was still in the bottom of the bag, she retrieved a pair of socks and jeans, the only clothes she'd kept in the hotel locker. She'd barely gotten the pant legs over her feet when the door handle rattled and she heard a frustrated growl coming from outside.

"Open the door." Phelan's demand was followed by the sound of his fist banging on the exterior.

"All right, give me a…" She tugged her pants up to her hips and worked on the zipper as she moved through the room.

Wood cracked and the chair splintered right before

Phelan shoved the door open.

Tessa froze. She glared at the demolished chair, then back at him. "You couldn't wait two more seconds?"

He crossed his arms. "Why did you try to keep me out?"

Keep him out? What has gotten into him? She could understand his behavior when he was trying to protect her. Given their history, this was an extremely possessive act and totally out of character for him. Her wolf, the fickle bitch, was enjoying his assertive actions and wanted more of his attention. Tessa, on the other hand, wasn't impressed.

"If you hadn't noticed, the locks are ruined, and it wouldn't stay shut." She hooked the button on her jeans, smiling smugly when his attention was drawn to the movement. "I wanted to get dressed without being ogled by the half-naked jerk hanging around outside."

"Sorry." He closed the door and glanced at the destruction he'd caused. Grabbing a splintered chair leg, he jammed it along the base to keep it shut.

Tessa went into the bathroom, grabbed her socks, shoes, and backpack. When she turned around, Phelan was standing in the doorway. "Want to explain to me what you're doing here? And what is going on with you and the jackals?" There was still an edginess in his voice, but some of the anger had subsided.

Not really. "It's a long story, and one I doubt you will believe." She was still having a hard time believing it. She squeezed past him, dropped the bag on the floor, and sat on the edge of the bed. "Why don't you tell me why *you're* here and not Logan?"

He crossed his arms and leaned against the wall. "I was asked to find you and bring you back to the hotel."

"Thanks for the rescue." A part of her was hoping he'd come after her because he wanted to, not because he was following orders from his alpha. A little disappointed, she pulled on her socks, then slipped on her shoes. "How did you know where to find me?"

"I have my methods." He flashed her a devilish grin, then took a seat next to her on the bed. "You can't keep evading my questions."

Actually, she could. She might not be able to shift, but her wolf wasn't passive. She had the same strengths as any alpha in their human form. Something Phelan had yet to learn.

"I know you stole something from Draven. Care to enlighten me as to why?"

"How did you…" She groaned, finally remembering the new camera Zach had recently installed. "You and Logan saw me on the security feeds."

He nodded without elaborating.

"Technically, I didn't *steal* anything." She had borrowed, more like rescued, the pendant to save Nira.

He quirked a brow. "This is serious." He brushed his hand along her arm, causing her to shudder.

Tell me something I don't know.

"Those men tried to kill you." His concern soothed her wolf, made her want to reach for him, find safety in his embrace. "I can't help you if you don't tell me what is going on." He ran his hand over his face. "Whatever it is, you can trust me. I want to help."

Tessa shifted sideways and studied the genuine sincerity on his face. She wanted so badly to believe him, but she couldn't. The man had literally gone out of his way to avoid her for months. Now, because he'd saved her life, he expected her to believe he wasn't just doing his job and she could trust him. Trust didn't come easily to her. She'd learned the hard way what relying on others would cost her.

No, if he wanted her to open up to him, he'd have to earn it. Simply saying the words didn't count. "Who said I wanted your help?" She snatched her backpack off the floor and secured the zipper. "You can take me back to the hotel."

"I'm taking you to division headquarters."

"What...you said..."

"I said Logan ordered me to find you," Phelan said.

"Fine, then I'll walk." She pushed off the bed and tugged the strap of her bag over her shoulder.

Phelan got to his feet and blocked her path to the door. "Stealing is a crime." He moved closer. Close to the point of intimidating.

She held her ground, fighting the urge to put some distance between them.

"Since you won't tell me what I want to know, I'm going to take you to the station and lock you up for your own protection." He ran his thumb along her jaw and grinned. "At least until we can sort this out."

"Are you kidding me?" By his stern expression, she knew he meant every word. Panicked, Tessa took a step back. The idea of being caged agitated her wolf, and she snarled. Her human side, the part of her that suffered from claustrophobia, wasn't happy about it either.

Being locked up also meant she couldn't search for Nira, and that was unacceptable. No way was she going to accompany him or allow him to detain her. "We'll see what Logan has to say about that." Reaching into one of the outside pockets of her pack, she retrieved her phone.

She'd didn't get a chance to turn it back on before he snatched the phone from her hand. "Hey. Give that back." Tessa wanted to wrestle it away from him and wipe the satisfied smirk off his face at the same time. "What do you think you're doing?"

CHAPTER EIGHT

Screw the last six months of restraint, of holding back because Tessa was his partner's sister, was his alpha's niece. Phelan wasn't letting her out of his sight. At least not now, and maybe not ever if his wolf had anything to say about it.

Being stubborn and willful must be a Kern family trait. A trait that obviously hadn't bypassed Tessa. Judging by the way she clenched her jaw, Phelan had a feeling she'd punch him long before she'd tell him what he wanted to know. She was rather good at evasion. The fact that she'd been so convincing and had been able to elude him at the casino earlier had bruised his ego. And, if he was being honest, it had royally pissed him off.

It hadn't been a surprise that she balked when he asked her to trust him. She didn't know him all that well, not her fault, his. She'd been nothing but warm and friendly from the moment he'd been introduced to the pack. She'd even offered to show him around the city. It was a genuine welcome-to-the-pack kind of offer, not an I-want-to-get-you-into-my-bed kind of proposition. Not like the incident with Tanzy. After the way that mistake had affected his job, he'd been determined to avoid the female relatives of anyone he worked with, especially Tessa.

Reflecting on his actions over the last few months, she had every right not to believe he was being sincere. He'd been a rude jerk in his attempts to avoid her, and now it was biting him in the ass. Damn if it didn't bother him and weigh him down with guilt.

He slid her phone into his back pocket. "You've committed a crime, and that falls under the division's jurisdiction. Logan no longer has any say in the matter." Of course, he was bluffing. His alpha would have his hide if he locked her up without talking to him first, but she didn't need to know that. When Logan received his text letting him know he'd found her, he responded by telling Phelan not to bring her back to the hotel. Not until they knew what was going on and thought it was safe.

There was a good chance Logan would already be at the station by the time Phelan arrived with Tessa. It upset Phelan that she wouldn't talk to him. Maybe her uncle would have better luck, and for some reason, that irritated him even more.

The unrelenting tightness in his chest was a constant reminder of how close he'd come to losing her. He hated resorting to intimidation but she'd left him no choice. Her safety was the force driving his decisions, and he couldn't protect her if he had no clue what was going on. All shifters feared being trapped. Since she wasn't willing to give him answers freely, he'd hoped the threat of being caged would encourage her to talk.

"There's no way I'm going anywhere with you."

So much for intimidation. "I would prefer you go willingly, but I if you don't..."

"If I don't, then what?" She stuck out her chin and crossed her arms defiantly.

"Then I'll be forced to toss you over my shoulder and spank you." Something he was tempted to do anyway. Not because he was angry, but because he'd been admiring her backside for a long time and wanted to know how it would feel in the palm of his hand.

"You wouldn't dare."

"Trust me, I would. Especially, after the stunt you pulled when you promised me you'd stay in the break room."

She cringed at this words, then glared at him, her wolf making its presence known by darkening the smoky gray in her eyes. "Fine. Can I at least use the bathroom first?"

"By all means." He didn't want her to think he was a complete asshole. "I'll wait for you outside." He should have known better than to turn his back on her. Should have suspected she'd try something when she'd agreed to accompany him so easily. Phelan realized his mistake the minute he felt something hard connect with his head.

Pain radiated across the back of his skull. "Son of a…" He groaned and stumbled forward, dropping to the floor. This wasn't the first time he'd received a blow to the head, and he was certain it wouldn't be the last. Luckily, she hadn't hit him hard enough to render him unconscious. Shifters were tough. It took a lot more than being smacked over the head to do any real damage—a fact she had to know.

Phelan could understand her being nervous after he'd threatened to lock her up, but this…this was excessive. Smelling her fear, he realized something else was motivating her reaction, and he had every intention of finding out what it was. He wasn't worried that she'd get far. He was fast and could catch her effortlessly. Keeping his eyes closed and his breathing even, he remained perfectly still and patiently waited to see what she'd do next.

"Phelan, I'm so sorry." He sensed Tessa beside him right before she poked his shoulder.

She wedged her hand into his front pocket, rubbing his hip, grazing his groin, and making him hard. It took everything he had not to groan and reach for her. Finally, after a short, unbearable amount of time, she worked her fingers around his keys and removed her hand.

#

When he wakes up, he's going to kill me. Tessa gripped Phelan's keys, trying to keep her hands from shaking. She knew he would never purposely hurt her. Logan and Ryland always spoke highly of him and respected his loyalty to the pack.

She couldn't believe she'd panicked. After the stress of being attacked, trying to save Nira, and keeping her family safe, the threat of being caged was more than she could take. Living with a wolf that'd been trapped her entire life only made it worse.

Dealing with an erratic mother had taught her how to guard her emotions and handle all the difficult things life tossed at her as rationally as possible. She *DID NOT* react emotionally, and she certainly didn't thwack handsome, absolutely mouthwatering, gorgeous guys over the head with lamps.

Phelan did more than make her mouth water. The attraction she had for him was different from any other man she'd met. He drew her and her wolf on a level she didn't understand and couldn't begin to explain.

Caressing the back of his head where she'd hit him with the lamp, she flinched when her fingertips skimmed over a lump. "I'm so, so sorry." She knew she was repeating herself, but she couldn't help it. Phelan was breathing, and logically, she knew he was fine. Shifters could take a lot more pain than humans and had superior healing powers. At most, he'd wake up with a hellacious headache. "You didn't give me any choice."

Figuring she'd never get another opportunity, Tessa placed her face against his neck and inhaled his scent. Something she'd wanted to do from the first time she'd met him. *Damn, he smells good.* Spicy, sandalwood, male—a tantalizing aroma that had her melting from the inside out.

"I wish I could trust you…" Uncertain why she felt the need to explain herself, especially since he couldn't hear her, she continued, "I need to help…people I care about could get hurt…you wouldn't understand." The not-understanding part was more a confession about her secret than anything else. She brushed her lips across the short stubble on his jaw and placed a soft kiss on his cheek. With a regretful sigh, she got to her feet.

She grabbed her backpack, then carefully stepped around him. She'd barely taken a step toward the door when she felt tight clamps around her ankles. Rooted in place but too late to stop the momentum, she released a high-pitched squeal and fell forward.

Within seconds, Phelan was on top of her and had flipped her onto her back. He straddled her hips with his thick thighs and used one hand to pin her arms above her head. "What were you going to do with these? Steal my truck?" He pulled the keys out of her grasp and slipped them into his pocket.

"I told you I'm not a thief. I would have had Logan send someone back for you as soon as I got to the hotel."

He rubbed the back of his head. "That wasn't nice." His tone didn't carry the anger she'd expected. In fact, warmth flickered in his dark gaze, and he appeared to be amused.

"You shouldn't have threatened to… Get off me." She dug her heels into the carpet and tried bucking him off. A wasted effort since he was bigger and weighed a lot more than she did.

Her wolf rather enjoyed being in close proximity to him and couldn't comprehend why Tessa was having a problem with it.

"No, not until you talk to me." His voice was low, soothing, seductive. He used one hand to keep her arms locked in place and pushed some loose curls off her cheek.

"What wouldn't I understand?"

The sneaky bastard. "You were awake the whole time, weren't you?" Tessa felt a wave of heat surge along her throat and cheeks. He'd heard everything she said, knew she'd sniffed his neck. And kissed him. Why did she have to kiss him? Her stupid wolf, unlike her, was actually prancing and acting smug about it.

If there was ever a time she wished the floor would open up and swallow her, now was it.

#

"My head's pretty tough. You didn't hit me very hard." Phelan found her embarrassment adorable and grinned when her cheeks flushed a deep pink and she nervously bit her lip. A lip he'd love to be nibbling on himself.

"I'll make a note for next time." Her teasing laughter filled the air.

Phelan couldn't believe she'd scented him, then brushed her lips along his jaw. The gentle kiss was an intimate and possessive act, and had him and his wolf going crazy. It had been bad enough to spend the last few months fighting his yearning for her from a distance. With her this close, the alluring blend of honey and coconut mixed with her arousal was making him hard.

He was so close to losing control and taking her right there on the floor. He had no common sense when it came to Tessa. If he did, he'd put some distance between them, turn her over to Ryland and let him deal with her. Instead, like an idiot, he decided to tempt fate and lowered his mouth over her lips. He didn't simply sample. No, he conquered, devoured, owned, and left her no doubt she'd been thoroughly kissed.

She shuddered and moaned, her response receptive and filled with a vigor that matched his own. Reluctantly, he ended the kiss, searching the desire in her gaze for any hint that he'd gone too far. *What is wrong with me?* He was supposed to be protecting her, trying to get answers, not seduce her on a hotel floor.

"If I let you up, will you promise to behave?" Now that she seemed more relaxed, not so edgy, he might be able to get some answers.

"I…"

The ringtone he'd assigned to Logan filled the air, interrupting her response. If it had been anyone else, he'd be tempted to ignore it. Logan was waiting for them at the station, had expected them to be there already, and was probably worried they'd run into more problems.

Phelan released her wrist and straightened to retrieve his phone. "Logan." He struggled to keep his irritation under control.

"Is Tessa all right? Where are you?" Logan growled.

"She's fine." *More than fine.* Phelan grinned when Tessa squirmed and rolled her eyes. He knew with her wolf's enhanced senses she could hear both sides of the conversation. "We had a slight delay, but we'll be there shortly." He ended the call and returned his phone to his pocket.

"Time to go." Reluctantly, he rolled to the side, then helped her to her feet.

Tessa frowned and punched him in the chest.

"What was that for?" He rubbed the spot where she'd nailed him with her fist. If she hit him because he'd kissed her, she'd be waiting a long time—like forever—for an apology. He had no regrets.

"You never had any intention of locking me up, did you?" She fisted her hand as if preparing to swing at him again.

"Kind of makes us even." He grabbed her wrist, massaging her hand with his thumb until she relaxed her fingers.

Understanding dawned in her expression, and he knew she figured out that he was referring to her fib about staying put earlier. Surprisingly, she smiled. "Yeah, I guess it does."

"We should get going." Phelan leaned forward and snagged her backpack off the ground only to have her quickly snatch it away from him and tug the strap over her shoulder. By the way she protectively clutched the bag, he wondered if she had Draven's pendant hidden inside. He'd thought about asking her to produce it, then decided to wait until they met with Logan. As much as he'd enjoyed seeing her riled, he wasn't thrilled about having her take another swing at his head. He preferred having her cooperation.

He removed the piece of wood holding the door in place, then stepped back, allowing her to go first.

"What, don't trust me?" She glanced at the lamp and grinned wickedly before heading out of the room.

Phelan chuckled. "Not even a little."

CHAPTER NINE

Phelan kept his hand pressed against the small of Tessa's back as he led her along the busy hallway at division headquarters. Instead of taking her to his office, a medium-sized cubicle with two desks that he shared with Ryland, he led her in the direction of the interrogation rooms.

He was glad when he sensed some of her tension had disappeared. She'd been quiet and wary since they'd arrived, and he suspected she still believed he planned to lock her in a cell. If not for Logan's request, he wouldn't have brought her here. He would have taken her someplace safe, like his home. Maybe even into his bed.

"Tessa," a male voice called from behind them.

She stopped and glanced over her shoulder. "Hey, Vince." She flashed the wolf shifter, another pack member and fairly recent division recruit, a bright smile as he sauntered toward them. "How are you doing?" She let Vince pull her into a hug.

It annoyed Phelan at how easily she accepted the other man's embrace. His wolf didn't understand the social niceties. All he saw was a male touching the female he believed belonged to him. His animal growled and anxiously paced, ready to attack.

"Wonderful now that you're here." He gave her a flirtatious wink and kept her close by loosely holding one of her hands.

Though Vince never openly acted on it, Phelan suspected the younger wolf had a thing for Tessa. The guy was always hovering and sniffing around her at their monthly pack meetings or the social events Logan sponsored. His wolf raised his hackles and snarled, insisting Phelan rip out the guy's throat out if he didn't stop touching Tessa. Phelan, the man, thought the animal made a good point. Before he could stop it, a rumble rose from deep in his chest, warning Vince to back off.

Vince immediately released her hand, submissively dropping his gaze as he took a cowering step backward. "Sorry, Phelan. I didn't know." He glanced at Tessa nervously, then pointed his thumb behind him. "I should probably get back to work. I'll talk to you later." He gave her a half smile, then turned and hurried down the hall.

Satisfied that Vince wouldn't be going anywhere near Tessa anytime soon, Phelan placed his hand on her elbow, urging her forward.

"What was that about?" She gazed at him curiously and refused to move.

"Nothing." Phelan didn't want to analyze his overprotective behavior too closely and wasn't in the mood to explain it to her.

"Uh-huh." Tessa reluctantly let him take her elbow again.

"We're in here." He showed her into the first room on the right. Other than the rectangular table and four chairs in the middle of the room, the small, white-walled area seemed sterile and confining. "Have a seat, and I'll go find Logan." Since Logan and Brock were close friends, he assumed he'd find him in his boss's office.

"Can I bring you anything on my way back? The coffee here isn't great, but the vending machine has a decent hot chocolate."

"I would love a cup." Tessa grinned. "I never would've taken you for a hot chocolate kind of guy."

"One of the many secrets behind my charming personality."

"Charming. Really?" She snorted her disbelief.

"A skeptic, eh?" Phelan grinned, enjoying the easy banter and her challenge. "I guess I'll have to prove it to you."

"You do that." Hearing Tessa's laughter touched him in a warm and welcoming way.

"Would you mind leaving the door open?" She warily took a seat in one of the two chairs on the opposite side of the table.

"You aren't planning to disappear on me, are you?" It troubled Phelan that she might run again. He hoped she trusted him enough to stay and let him help her.

"No. I'll stay here." She glanced around and swallowed hard. "I have a thing about enclosed spaces."

That explained why she'd smacked him over the head with the lamp. She hadn't been trying to get away from him, she was afraid of being caged. Phelan didn't know if he should feel relieved or guilty for threatening her.

He nodded and gave her a contemplative glance. She appeared exhausted and stressed. How long had it been since she'd gotten any sleep? "I'll be right back."

It didn't take him long to get their drinks and arrive at Brock's office. Even the vending machine, which had a nasty habit of stealing his money, seemed to understand his need to get back to Tessa. As he'd suspected, Logan was in the middle of an intense conversation with the bear. No doubt apprising him of the current situation with Draven.

Phelan figured it would be easier to avoid a lecture from Brock if he stayed out of his office. He tapped on the glass pane that served as part of the wall bordering the hallway. Both men glanced in his direction. Phelan expected Brock to yell and was surprised when all he got was one of his usual glares.

A few seconds later, Logan exited the office and joined Phelan. "Where's Tessa?"

"She's waiting in one of the interrogation rooms." Phelan tipped his head to the left.

"I'll meet you there," Logan said.

Phelan hadn't made it far when a male's loud roar shook the same pane of glass he'd been peering through. He glanced over his shoulder to see Grant Fowler, furious and stalking toward Brock's office. "My parking lot is a media circus. I want to know what division is doing to find those responsible for dumping that woman on *my* property."

Damn, what is it with bears and bellowing? Brock might not be as tall or as broad as Grant, but Phelan was willing to bet the black bear wouldn't have any problem going head-to-head with the grizzly. He spent another minute watching the two men snarl at each other, then decided to put his money on Grant. He chuckled on his way back to Tessa. Yeah, he was definitely glad this wasn't his problem.

#

Seriously...an intervention. Tessa wanted to crawl under the table when Logan, Ryland, and Brayden, the three most intimidating and overbearing men in her family, entered the room. She choked on the hot chocolate Phelan had given her right before he took the seat on her left.

The Kern men were similar in appearance—tall, built, drool-worthy—yet completely different in personalities. It always astonished her how much raw animalistic power poured off them when they were together. Combine that with Phelan's intense energy and she was practically squirming in her seat.

"You okay?" Phelan patted her gently between the shoulder blades. As if sensing her discomfort, he leaned closer and kept his voice low so only she could hear him. "I didn't know they'd all be here." He remained close and showed his support by draping his arm across the back of her chair.

The attentive move surprised her, confused her, and reminded her of the kiss they'd shared earlier. Equally dominating, equally possessive. So different from the aloof behavior she'd come to expect from him. Had he been any other wolf, she'd push him away, challenge his right to be this close. Instead, she leaned back and accepted his touch, let his scent embrace her, soothe her.

If any of the other males noticed his behavior, and she was certain they did, none of them bothered to comment.

Tessa knew she had at least one supporter among her relatives. She glanced at Brayden, who was leaning against the opposite wall, arms crossed, his sympathetic gaze focused on her. She understood why Logan would want Ryland to be here but not why he requested the presence of his younger brother. Maybe his appearance had something to do with his employee. If Logan had seen her on the security footage as Phelan had said, then he'd know Rita had been entertaining Draven in the hot tub area. It was a good guess that she was no longer employed at the restaurant.

Ryland took a seat across from Phelan. Logan paced as if gathering his thoughts, then gripped the back of the remaining chair. "Would you like to tell me what is going on?" He narrowed his eyes and pinned her with a determined glare.

If Tessa had been anyone else in the pack, those words would have been emphasized with the full force of his alpha growl. Even with his less than intimidating tone, she still had to suppress the urge to cower. "It's going to sound crazy so I want your promise that you'll hear me out before making a hasty decision."

"Fine," Logan snarled and impatiently crossed his arms. "Go on."

Tessa inhaled deeply to gather her thoughts and decide the best place to start. "While I was dealing…"

"I want to see my daughter," a loud and familiar female voice boomed from the hallway, interrupting their conversation.

Oh, heck. Tessa didn't think things could possibly get any worse until the door burst open and revealed Margery Kern Shaw.

Vince grimaced and blocked the doorway, trying to keep her out. Her crazy mother could be more intimidating than ten alpha males combined. Tessa felt bad for the guy. No one could stop her mother when she made up her mind to do something.

"Sorry, she…" Vince aimed an apologetic gaze at Logan.

"It's okay. Let her in." Logan didn't appear happy to see Margery either.

"Mom, what are you…" Tessa glanced at Ryland, who'd vacated his chair and was nervously shifting from one foot to the other. "You called her, didn't you?" She shot her brother a glare that promised retribution later.

Ryland shrugged, suddenly finding the floor more interesting than meeting her gaze.

"Of course, he called me. I'm your mother." There was an accusatory tone in her voice. "Why didn't you call me?" She pushed past Logan and sat in the empty chair. "If you've gotten yourself into trouble again…I want to help."

There was no such thing as help from her mother. Margery's idea of assisting was making a situation far worse than it had been to begin with. It was the last thing Tessa wanted. Glancing at the males in her family, she hoped to find some assistance. Their blank expressions confirmed that they had no intention of interfering. Interfering meant drawing Margery's full attention. And Tessa knew from experience the cowards would do anything to avoid dealing with her wrath. The sooner she was allowed to deliver whatever rant had wound her up, the sooner she'd leave.

Tessa tightened her grip on the backpack sitting in her lap and braced for the lecture she knew was coming.

"Now, tell me what you did this time?" Margery propped her elbows on the table and clasped her hands together, expectantly waiting for an answer.

"It's not what you think." Tessa hated that her mother made it sound as if visiting her daughter at the station was a regular part of her routine.

"How can it not be what I think?" Margery waved her had around the room. "You're here. The boys are here. Tell us what you did so we can get back to our busy lives."

There was no point in arguing. Margery was a master at dramatics. She had a knack for implying that everything Tessa did was aimed at disrupting her life.

"I don't need any more grief." Right on cue, Margery sniffled. "If you aren't going to cooperate, then I have no choice but to ground you."

Tessa massaged her forehead, trying to ease the dull throb. It wouldn't be long before she had another headache. "You do realize I'm not ten years old anymore, right? You can't ground me."

Margery's serious glare said she believed she damned well could. "I blame her father for this." She smiled sweetly at Phelan. "I should have known better than to get involved with a magician." Her appreciative gaze swept over him as if she were considering him for the position of her next husband.

Tessa couldn't remember if Margery was working on number four or five. She'd stopped counting after three. "Mom," Tessa said through gritted teeth. Mother or not, she would claw the woman's skin off if she dared to make a move on Phelan.

"Did you know she has a criminal record?" Margery sighed heavily and placed a hand over her chest as if she'd given birth to a serial killer.

Here we go. Tessa groaned inwardly. One stupid mistake,

one little joyride, and she was marked as a criminal for life. A joyride instigated by Aurelia. Her cousin was the one who'd supposedly taken the car to get even with her cheating boyfriend. A fact she'd neglected to share with Tessa until after they'd been picked up by the cops. Since she was over eighteen and had been in the car at the time, she'd gained a black mark on her record. A black mark her mother would never let her forget.

Maybe she could find a way to add this to her long list of reasons why it would be okay to strangle Aurelia once she got out of this mess. Maybe she should rephrase that to *if...if she got out of this mess.* Right now, things weren't going in her favor.

"Baby, you know your father is the reason you can't shift." Margery's pout lacked any real sympathy.

"Thanks, *Mom.*" Tessa ground her teeth. "Not everyone in the room was aware of that fact." She glanced at Phelan, expecting to see disgust. To have him put some distance between them. Instead, he lightly stroked her shoulder. The action pleased and placated her irritated wolf.

Generally, shifters who couldn't transform were considered broken, not worthy of attention. They definitely weren't relationship material or desirable enough to be claimed as a mate. A part of Tessa was thankful she hadn't met her destined match. It was better never knowing him than to spend the rest of her life living with his rejection.

Margery waved her hand through the air dismissively. "Pfft. Phelan's your brother's partner. He's practically family." Her mother glanced at the silver watch on her wrist, one of the many expensive gifts she'd received from ex-husband number two. The custom-designed piece had four small diamonds crafted around the face and was proof that her mother loved expensive things. "I have to be going, and I don't want to hear from anyone else how you've gone back to your criminal ways."

"For the last time, I am not a criminal. Aurelia is the one…"

Margery got to her feet. "You need to stop blaming your cousin for your problems." She leaned across the table and kissed Tessa on the forehead, then headed for the door. "I'll call you later."

Tessa shook her head, making a mental note to monitor her phone's caller ID. She fully intended to avoid the woman for the next few days.

As soon as the door closed, Ryland chuckled. If they'd been alone, Tessa would have wiped the smirk off his face. No matter. She was a patient person, and knowing she could, and would, get even later eased some of her humiliation. "I can't believe you called her."

Ryland's smile disappeared, replaced by worry. "Come on. We were all worried about you. I only called her to see if she knew where you were. I had no idea she'd come down here."

"How did she know I was here?"

"I, uh…" Ryland stammered.

Oh yeah, I have him. Tessa smiled, letting her vicious side surface. They might have different fathers, but they were a lot closer than most of the other siblings she knew. Playing pranks on each other was something they'd done since they were children. Even if she never followed through on her threat, it would be fun watching Ryland squirm for the next few weeks wondering what she was going to do to retaliate.

"If you two are done screwing around, can we get back to your explanation?" Powerful, angry vibes from Logan's wolf swirled around the room, demanding their full attention.

Tessa sank back in her seat. She had a dreadful feeling this was going to be a lot worse than any of the scenarios she'd imagined.

#

Phelan and the other men in the room spent the next fifteen minutes listening intently to Tessa. She explained what had happened with Draven at the blackjack table, her experience with Nira, and why she'd taken the pendant. Every time she'd paused or glanced around the room, he sensed her apprehension and fear. And each time, ignoring the curious glances from the other males, he'd offer his support by rubbing her shoulder and encouraging her to continue.

By the time she was finished, his resolve to maintain some kind of distance from the sexy she-wolf had completely dissolved. Memories of their kiss, and the way her body had responded to his, continued to play through his thoughts, reinforcing his determination to keep her close. His wolf scratched and snarled, daring anyone to challenge his right to be near her.

Female shifters, especially wolves, were prickly when it came to being touched by unrelated males. He was mildly shocked she hadn't pushed him away. She was as responsive and accepting now as she had been when he'd kissed her. His wolf agreed with Phelan's refusal to break the connection.

He admired her strength of character and her determination to risk her own life to help a complete stranger. A stranger who was nothing more than a voice in her mind. Though he wished she'd confided in him, he now understood her motivation and was willing to do whatever it took to help her.

"I haven't been able to connect with Nira for a while now. She'd said her powers were weakening, and I'm worried something might be wrong." Tessa dug through her backpack and produced the pendant. The crimson stone surrounded by silver miniature talons had an ominous quality.

"May I?" Ryland, always the cop, took the pendant from her hand and examined it on both sides. "You honestly expect us to believe this contains a person's essence, a fairy no less?"

Out of the three males, Phelan wasn't surprised by Ryland's skepticism. His partner was one of those guys driven by hard facts. He didn't believe in something unless he could see it, touch it, taste it. Tessa's story was hard to imagine, but he couldn't believe she'd go to all this trouble based on something unrealistic.

He understood why Ryland would have his doubts. As a rule, shifters didn't associate with the witching community. Magicians were one thing; their low-level magic wasn't threatening or dangerous. Witches, the ones who were powerful and spiteful toward other magically enhanced beings, had been known to force his kind to remain in their animal forms, using them as subservient protectors against their enemies. No shifter with any sense would risk putting themselves in that position.

It would have taken a great deal of magical energy to trap Nira's essence in the pendant, which meant Draven had developed some sort of alliance with a witch. Powers like that came from dark magic, and there was always a price. Phelan wondered what the jackal wanted so badly that he was willing to make a deal with a witch. Worse, what had the jackal promised to deliver in return? Whatever *it* was, his instincts were screaming that it wasn't good.

"Yes, I…" Tessa snapped.

"Why not?" Brayden interrupted before Phelan could come to her rescue. Her uncle pushed away from the wall and snatched the pendant away from Ryland. "We all know other magical beings exist. Is it really a stretch to believe that this Nira person was able to tap into Tessa's empathetic powers?"

An empath, huh. Tessa must have inherited the ability from her father. Phelan wondered if it was the reason Margery blamed him for all her problems.

"Besides, when has Tessa ever done anything that

would put the family or the pack at risk?" Logan stepped forward and took the pendant from Brayden. He rubbed his hand down his face. "Why didn't you come to me first?" He handed the pendant back to Tessa, who quickly returned it to her backpack.

"Because I was afraid you wouldn't believe me. Or worse, you'd do the overprotective thing and lock me up and tell me it was for my own good." Tessa waved her hand around the room to emphasize that they'd done exactly what she'd predicted. "You never would have let me go after the pendant."

"Damned straight. Messing with jackals is dangerous." Ryland smacked the table. "You could have been killed, and it's our job to protect you."

"I'm not a child, and I can damn well take care of myself." Tessa gripped the backpack until her knuckles whitened. With all the anger pouring off her, Phelan was afraid she was going to fly across the table and throttle her brother.

"Tessa, honey, none of us think you're a child." Logan applied the same appeasing tone Phelan had heard him use when dealing with disputes between other pack members. He'd always admired the way the alpha led and protected his pack. "We know you can take care of yourself…"

"Good, then you won't try to stop me from finding Nira, right?" Tessa shot her uncle a look that said she thought he was full of shit and at the same time dared him to disagree with her.

Phelan found it amusing that Brayden covered his mouth, obviously trying to disguise a grin. Though the alpha's younger brother was protective of Tessa, Phelan had noticed Brayden was the only one of the three who always showed her support and didn't try to control her.

Phelan watched an array of emotions flit across Logan's face as he struggled with making the decision. He understood that Logan, as a family member, would want to protect her and keep her safe. He'd been dealing with the overwhelming urges ever since he found her with Draven. He had a feeling her mother's constant berating was already a source of contention for Tessa.

Having the males in her life dismiss her usefulness or her abilities would cause unnecessary animosity and more than likely undermine her self-worth. "I'll help her." Part of Phelan's reason for volunteering was because he didn't want Tessa to get hurt. Selfishness was his main motivator. He simply wanted to keep her close and was willing to do whatever was necessary to make it happen.

"What?" Astonished, Ryland and Logan responded at the same time.

Brayden refrained from commenting. He flashed Phelan an appreciative grin, then went back to leaning against the wall.

"Tessa's right. We need her." Phelan returned Logan's questioning gaze. "She's the only one who can communicate with Nira, and we can't allow Draven to execute his plan."

"I agree with Phelan," Brayden chimed in. "The solstice is in two days, and the jackals aren't going to stop searching for her or the pendant." He glared at Logan. "What were you going to do? Keep her locked in a jail cell until then?"

"Well, I…" Logan's averted gaze and the red flush above his shirt collar confirmed that he'd considered the option.

"She can stay at my place." Phelan struggled to remain serious. The thought of having Tessa in his home held a lot of appeal and pleased his wolf. "I have two spare guest rooms, and my house has extra security." Because he valued his privacy, he'd specifically chosen a home within a shifters-only community. The house was located along the perimeter and offered him access to an isolated area for his wolf to run when he shifted. He'd have her where he wanted her and be able to keep her safe at the same time.

#

"Hold on, don't I get a say in this?" Tessa glanced suspiciously around the room, studying each of the men in her family before locking her gaze with Phelan. She was thankful he'd kept them from locking her up, their version of protecting her, but she also wondered if he had an ulterior motive.

Their resounding "no" made Tessa cringe. It was no less than she'd expected.

"Work with me. I'm trying not to be a controlling male, but I need to know you're safe." Logan released a heavy sigh and scratched at the stubble on his chin. Exhaustion from the long hours he'd put in at work showed in the darkened skin below his eyes. Dealing with the threat of a jackal in his territory definitely couldn't be helping. "Locked in a room at the hotel or staying with Phelan. Your choice."

Tessa wasn't happy with either option. Given their history, or the lack of a substantial one, she was a little reluctant to accept Phelan's offer. On the other hand, Logan agreeing to have him protect her showed a level of trust in the man that she couldn't ignore.

Okay, so maybe staying with him wouldn't be so bad. She had to admit the prospect of being in his home, spending time alone with him, did sound enticing. It might also be responsible for the heat powering through her as if she'd stepped inside a furnace. Her wolf was delighted by the proposal and wasn't finding any problems with it whatsoever. Tessa swore if the damned animal was a cat she'd be purring.

"Fine, I'll stay with Phelan." At least outside of the hotel and the watchful eye of her family, she wouldn't feel so trapped. If for some reason Phelan changed his mind about letting her help, it would be a lot easier to get away from him. At least that was what she'd keep telling herself.

As soon as she agreed, the tense energy radiating off

the males and chipping away at her emotional shield faded. She wasn't sure how long the reprieve would last once she told them about the syringe. "You might want to show this to Brock." She unzipped the side pouch on her pack, retrieved the syringe, and placed it on the table in front of Logan.

"What's this?" Logan eyed it curiously, then returned to holding her gaze. "Where did you get it?"

"It's some kind of truth serum created by a witch. Supposedly, once the victim answers any questions they're asked, the magic fries them from the inside out."

"And how do you know that?" Ryland asked.

"One of the guys who attacked me, Gregor, I think, told me right before he tried to stick it in my arm."

Tessa felt Phelan's grip on her shoulder tighten, not enough to cause any pain, but enough to let her know that what she'd said had upset him.

"They were going to use this on you?" Logan growled, and his wolf's fury flashed in his eyes, a deadly glare letting everyone know he was ready to kill something. She glanced at Ryland and Brayden and could tell they were having similar reactions.

"Relax. I'm fine. They didn't hurt me." Tessa knew she was wasting her breath. Afraid Logan might change his mind about trusting her care to Phelan, she quickly added, "Phelan stopped them." She gripped his thigh under the table, urging him to back her up.

"She's right. I got there before they could use it." The word "barely" hung silently in the air between them.

"Thank you," Logan said. "We are in your debt." The three males all gave Phelan a brief nod, a sign that he'd earned their respect and gratitude.

"Have either of you ever seen anything like this before?" Logan directed his question to Phelan and Ryland.

"No, this is the first time I've come across it," Ryland said, shaking his head.

"My old unit came across magically enhanced serums before, but nothing this toxic or lethal." Phelan ran his hand along the back of his neck.

"You mentioned that one of them was named Gregor? Did you happen to get a last name?" Ryland directed his question to Tessa.

"No, though he called the other guy Kynan. And they were twins, if that helps."

"It might, though without last names, it will be a lot harder to find any information on them." Ryland tapped the table's surface.

"So what do we do now?" Her wolf's metabolism had already burned off the small amount of energy she'd gotten from the hot chocolate. Even though she was hungry, exhausted, and wanted to find a place to curl up and sleep, she wouldn't let it stop her if they were going to search for Nira.

"You will be staying put while we..." Logan motioned to everyone but Tessa. "Have a discussion with Brock and see where he is with finding Draven."

Tessa clamped her lips together tightly, resisting the urge to argue.

"I'll stay with Tessa while you three have a chat with Brock," Brayden, always taking on the diplomatic role, offered.

"Thanks." She smiled warmly at her uncle. Brayden probably volunteered in order to keep Logan from pulling a division officer into the room to babysit her. Something he knew would upset her.

"We shouldn't be gone too long." Phelan got to his feet and snatched the syringe off the table. When he reached the doorway, he hesitated and gave her one last glance before following Ryland and Logan into the hallway.

CHAPTER TEN

Once Logan, Ryland, and Phelan entered the office, Brock closed the wooden door, then lowered the white aluminum blind to cover the glass panel and prevent unwanted attention from the outside hallway. He sauntered behind the desk that swallowed up half the space in the small room, then plopped his large body into the chair, causing the joints to creak.

"What did you find out?" He directed his attention to Logan, who was sitting next to Ryland in one of the two chairs on the opposite side of the desk.

"Enough to know we have a serious problem but not enough to explain why," Logan said, the strain wearing on his features.

Phelan had chosen to stand and was perched on the edge of a lateral filing cabinet with a side view of all three men. He stared at the syringe in his hand and frowned. Tessa was definitely a distraction. It wasn't like him to overlook important details. After he'd gone in pursuit the twins and returned to her room, he'd been so preoccupied with Tessa he'd completely forgotten about the syringe.

While he waited for Logan to fill in Brock about the jackals, he studied the glowing green liquid. What little information they had so far wasn't nearly enough as far as he was concerned. Since there were several shifter-owned hotels in Vegas, Phelan didn't believe it was a coincidence Draven had shown up at the Fox and Hound. It bothered him that they still had no idea what the jackal was after and why he might be targeting the Kerns.

As soon as there was a pause in the conversation, Phelan glanced at Ryland and asked, "Do you think there's a connection between this..." He held up the syringe. "And the woman we found near Woodland Acres?" He glanced at Brock and raised a brow, daring him to bark at him for disobeying the order not to show up at the crime scene. The bear shot him a reproachful glare but remained silent. Either Logan had fulfilled his promise and talked to his boss, or the man was waiting to yell at Phelan once he got him alone.

"Marina did mention a strange green tint to the woman's skin," Ryland said.

"Did she have any idea what caused it?" Brock shoved aside a stack of files and propped his elbows on the desk.

"No, she said we'd have to wait until they got the results from the examiner." Phelan was afraid it might be a couple days before they got their answer, which wouldn't be soon enough to help them with the Nira situation. "Maybe Ryland can give her a call and see if she can expedite the process." Phelan, thankful his partner couldn't reach him, chuckled when he shifted uncomfortably in his seat and furiously glared at him.

"That's a good idea. Let me know what you find out." Brock was either oblivious to Ryland's reaction or he knew something about his history with Marina and wanted to screw with him.

Even though Phelan imagined the reprieve would be brief, he was glad to have the gruff bear messing with someone else's life for a change. "I'll drop this off with the lab boys for analysis, see if they can give us a better idea what we're dealing with." The two technicians on staff were both magicians and highly skilled. They would know how to handle whatever enchantment they found in the liquid.

"Anything on Draven since we spoke earlier?" Logan directed his question to Brock.

"I sent a couple of my best trackers to find him. So far they haven't found any trace of him since he left your hotel," Brock said.

"Do you think he's found a way to cover his scent?" Phelan remembered wondering why he hadn't been able to detect Draven from the minute he'd entered the casino. Even with all the different smells, his wolf wouldn't have a problem discerning the jackal from the rest of them.

He hadn't caught the jackal's scent until he'd gotten closer to Tessa's table. By then, Draven had unsheathed his claws and was on the verge of a shift. Was it possible the jackal found a way to conceal his scent until his animal started to emerge?

"It wouldn't be much of a leap to assume it was possible. If he's dealing with a witch, she could have provided him with some sort of enchantment." Brock snarled and smacked the desk. "I want her found. The last thing we need is one practicing dark magic in the city."

Phelan rubbed the tense muscles in his neck. "I did get a license plate number from the car the twins were driving. I have Vince running it now. Maybe we'll get lucky and can find Draven that way." He didn't hold out much hope the information would lead them anywhere. The jackal had done a good job of covering his trail so far. Phelan would bet the number on the plate was a fake or they'd discover the car was stolen.

"Any luck on Draven's history?" Brock glanced at Ryland.

"I'm still waiting to hear back from my contact in Arizona. Probably won't know anything until tomorrow, though," Ryland said.

"What about Tessa? I know you've a lot going on with

all the shows in the city." Brock tapped his fingertips on the desk's surface. "We can offer her protection if you need the assistance."

Rationally, Phelan knew Brock's offer had merit. The black bears owned a small community on the outskirts of the city. Their pack, more formally called a sleuth, might be smaller than the wolves', but they were just as tough when one of their own was threatened. Tessa was well liked by the grouchy older bear and fell into that category.

Considering their current relationship, Phelan figured Brock would refuse out of spite. He tensed and fought back a growl, prepared to argue, fight if necessary, should that happen.

Before he could dispute Brock's proposal, Logan interjected, "I appreciate the offer, but Phelan will be taking care of her."

Again, Phelan was surprised to hear the level of trust expressed in his alpha's confident words. He wondered if Logan would be so supportive if he knew his interest in Tessa went way beyond merely keeping her safe.

Phelan's jaw nearly dropped when Brock acquiesced with a nod of approval. *I'll be damned.*

"Are you going to require any additional security at the hotel?" Brock seemed to have come to the same conclusion Logan had earlier. If Draven posed a threat to the Kerns, eventually there would be bloodshed. Logan's family, the employees, even their guests could be at risk.

"Not at the moment. We plan to keep the news about the jackals as quiet as possible until we know why he's here and what his intentions are." Logan might appear calm, but his underlying stress pulsed through the room. "If the situation changes, I'll let you know." He glanced at Phelan. "You should get Tessa out of here. After being in that room all this time, her wolf is probably going crazy."

#

If Tessa didn't get out of the small, growing smaller by the minute, interrogation room, she was going to lose it. Being crammed into the confining space and keeping her shield in place had been a struggle. The men in her family had a tendency to forget their wolves pulsated with power. Combine that with their human emotions and it was a miracle she wasn't screaming.

As soon as Logan, Ryland, and Phelan left the room, she took several reassuring breaths to convince her wolf they weren't really caged and could leave whenever they wanted. Any headway she'd made disappeared when Brayden closed the door and approached her in three long strides.

He bypassed the chair and parked his rear on the corner of the table blocking her view of the exit. "How are you doing?" Concern flickered in his cognac-colored eyes and helped ease some of her trepidation.

"Tired, cranky, and in need of food." She wanted to add sex to her list but held her tongue. After spending what seemed like forever sitting next to Phelan, feeling his touch, and taking in his tantalizing scent, she was definitely beyond a little frustrated.

Brayden gave her one of his understanding smiles. *Damn observant wolf.* Seeing those dimples and knowing he'd guessed what she'd been thinking sent a flush of heat to her cheeks. Despite her close bond with this particular uncle, sex was not a subject she readily discussed with him. The only time the topic came up was when she was teasing him about one of his many short-lived relationships.

Besides the natural animal magnetism of his wolf and his boyish charm, Brayden was a six-foot package of firm muscles and powerful male. From what Tessa had seen, most of the women drawn to him were superficial, lacked any real intelligence or substance, and seemed to suit his current lifestyle. They were more like flings or conquests since none of them lasted longer than a few weeks. The latest was a model named Diane, or maybe it was Darcy?

Tessa had a hard time keeping track.

Though his reasons for avoiding a long-term commitment were different from hers, like her, he refused to let anyone get too close. Tessa had already resigned herself to the fact that finding a mate, someone who accepted her the way she was, would probably never happen. It didn't mean she couldn't hold out hope for her uncle. Eventually, the right woman would come along and break through his well-constructed barriers and discover the great guy hidden underneath.

"I'd offer to get you something out of the vending machine, but I'm guessing you're in need of something with a little more substance."

Tessa nodded, thinking that a hamburger and a large plate of fries covered in ketchup would absolutely do the trick. The reminder had her stomach grumbling. She placed a hand over her midsection and groaned.

Brayden chuckled. "We'll see if we can get that taken care of once the guys come back."

After a long moment of silence, Tessa shot him a quizzical look. "So, no lecture? No, *what the heck were you thinking?*"

"Being judgmental is Logan's thing, not mine. You know that." He swiped his fingers through his hair and scratched his scalp. "I'm more interested to hear about what's up with you and Phelan."

"I don't know what you're talking about." Playing dumb with Brayden never worked, but she was in no mood to discuss the sexy male who'd been acting out of character since he'd rescued her.

The truth was she had no idea what was going on with Phelan. No idea why her shoulder still tingled from his warm touch. No idea why she'd enjoyed having him twirl her hair around his finger. Worse, she had no idea why she'd let him. In the past, if any shifter other than the members of her family had purposely gotten into her personal space without permission, she would have knocked them on their ass.

"Oh, come on. The guy didn't move more than two inches away from you the whole time he was in here." Brayden crossed his arms. "He was acting as possessive as a…"

Tessa threw up her hand. "Don't say it. We both know it's not possible. Not for me anyway." There would be no mate for her. No male wolf would want someone who was broken and couldn't shift. Refusing to let her uncle see her cry, she double blinked to stop the tears.

"Okay, sweetie." He rubbed his hand along her upper arm and gave her one of those looks that said he'd leave it alone. For now.

She quickly changed the subject. "I meant to ask, is Rita okay?" Tessa remembered how afraid she'd been for the human during her encounter with Draven.

"A little shaken up, but she'll be fine." Brayden's smile faded, replaced by a saddened expression.

"I take it she no longer works at the restaurant." Tessa knew Logan wouldn't stand for disloyalty, and Rita had abused their trust. Being human, she'd gotten off easy. If she'd been a pack member, losing her job would have been the least of her punishment.

"Yeah, and needless to say, Logan isn't too happy with me right now."

"He's blaming you for what Rita did."

Brayden nodded. "He thinks I should have known she was using the hot tub for her own personal pleasures."

"That's not fair. There was no way you could have known." Tessa might not agree with Logan's actions, but she understood them. He'd barely entered his twenties when his parents had died. Being the oldest male, he was tossed into the role of alpha and raising Brayden. Margery might have been older, but she was too immature and self-absorbed to offer much help. The responsibility of keeping his family together and running a large pack at such an early age had made Logan strong and powerful, but it had also hardened him.

Tessa adored her oldest uncle, yet she constantly worried about him. She'd never seen him take a break, step back from the throne, and take some time to relax. Brayden was the opposite. He was calm, laid-back, and enjoyed having fun. It was probably why the two of them clashed so much and why Logan was always chastising Brayden for his life choices.

"Fair or not, you know what it's like having an older brother." *Boy, do I.* Having that in common was another reason they were close. Ryland wasn't nearly as bad as Logan, but his overbearing, overprotective behavior could still be stifling.

There was a knock on the door, then Phelan walked into the room. "You ready to go?" He presented her with his usual frown, and Tessa wondered if he regretted his decision to act as her bodyguard.

"Sure." His gaze locked with hers, and she saw a longing she'd never noticed before. Heat swept across her skin, a wave of raw desire that left her tingling with need. How was she supposed to concentrate on finding Nira when all she wanted to do was pounce on the man? She wasn't alone. Her wolf was prancing, pushing her to rub him, scent him, and mark him as theirs.

Tessa blanked her expression and got to her feet, trying to appear indifferent and hoping her uncle hadn't noticed the sexual tension humming between them. "I'll talk to you later." She gave Brayden a quick hug and stepped past Phelan into the hallway.

"Hey, Phelan." Brayden had followed them from the room.

"Yeah."

"I'm counting on you to make sure Tessa doesn't get hurt." Brayden's statement had nothing to do with her safety. It was a warning that Phelan needed to tread carefully where her emotions were involved.

"I appreciate your concern…" Phelan returned the

threat with a growl and wrapped his hand possessively around her waist. "I'm sure she can take care of herself."

Brayden flashed an amused smile and winked at her.

Tessa groaned and threw her hands in the air. *Somebody save me from overprotective males.*

CHAPTER ELEVEN

Phelan hadn't gotten a chance to discuss anything with Tessa during the thirty minutes it had taken to reach his home. Five minutes after she'd snapped the seat belt into place and the truck was moving, she'd fallen asleep.

It was late afternoon by the time he'd swiped his access card on the panel near the security gate. He drove along the quiet streets to the rear of the complex, then pulled onto the concrete driveway in front of his double-car garage. His new home, a large two-story house with a light gray stucco and stone veneer exterior, was similar to the place he'd sold and left behind in San Diego.

While he waited for the electronic door to open, he glanced at Tessa. She appeared so beautiful, so peaceful, and he hated to wake her. He'd thought about carrying her inside and putting her to bed but he wasn't sure if she'd appreciate waking in a strange place.

Once the truck was parked inside, he turned in his seat. "Tessa, we're here." He brushed her cheek with the back of his hand and tucked the soft, dark curls behind her ear.

Slowly, her eyes fluttered open, and she straightened in her seat. "Sorry. I didn't mean to conk out on you." She offered him a weak smile.

"Don't be. When was the last time you got any sleep?"

She groggily glanced at the watch on her wrist. "Wow, not since yesterday morning."

"I'll bet you're hungry too."

"Starving, actually," she said.

"Let's go. I'll give you a quick tour after I make you something to eat." Phelan jumped out of the truck and reached her side as she was sliding out. He took her hand and tugged her toward the door leading into the house. "Afterward, you can get some more sleep."

"What about finding Nira?"

"There's not much we can do right now. Not until we learn more about Draven." He opened the door and led her into the living room. "A few hours of rest isn't going to change anything."

"You're probably right."

Phelan led her into the kitchen. "Have a seat." He pointed at the stools sitting next to the long counter in the center of the room. "Sandwiches okay?" He opened the refrigerator, glad he'd taken the time to go shopping a few days earlier.

"Sounds great, thanks." Tessa set her backpack on the floor and climbed onto a tall wooden stool.

He set a loaf of bread and a container filled with sliced meats and cheeses on the counter and worked on making their lunch.

"Just move in?" Tessa asked.

"A couple of months ago." He noticed Tessa staring at the stack of boxes piled in the corner of the dining room. "It's been a little busy at work. I haven't had much time to unpack."

"Uh, Phelan."

"Yeah." He stopped what he was doing and glanced at Tessa. She appeared to be struggling with what she wanted to say next. "Are you okay?"

She nodded. "I wanted to say thank you for helping me out with my family. They can be difficult." She bit her lower lip. "I was kind of surprised, you know, since I... How is your head, anyway?"

"All healed." He rubbed the back of his skull. "It's my ego that's still bruised, but if you'd like to kiss it and make it better..."

Tessa laughed. "I'm sure your ego will be fine."

"It was worth a try." He grinned and set two plates with sandwiches and chips on the counter, then grabbed two bottles of water from the refrigerator before taking the stool next to hers.

"Thank you."

"I'm not the greatest cook, but I do have a few skills."

"Good to know. I was worried you might starve me while I was here," she teased, and bit into her sandwich.

He grinned, loving her sense of humor. Being around her felt natural, comfortable, and the thought of her eventually leaving wasn't something he wanted to consider.

After they'd eaten in silence for a few minutes, Phelan asked, "Why don't you want anyone to know you're an empath?" He hadn't meant to blurt out the question, to sound so insensitive. Usually he had more tact and knew how to gradually work sensitive inquiries into a conversation.

"Isn't it obvious?" Tessa stiffened her shoulders and set her sandwich back on her plate. Her dejected tone tore at his heart.

"Should it be?" Judging by her reaction, her ability somehow caused her pain. Maybe not physically but definitely emotionally. And, like an idiot, he'd managed to upset her.

#

Phelan's question caught her off-guard. The only person who talked about Tessa's ability was her mother, and it was usually when Margery wanted to complain about her father.

"I'm sorry." He placed a comforting hand on her arm. "I'll understand if you don't want to talk about it."

"No, it's okay, I…"

"What?" Phelan raised his eyebrows and leaned toward her. Tessa let down her barriers enough to get a sampling of his emotions. There was no disgust, no hint that he judged her or thought less of her because she was different.

"Doesn't it make you uncomfortable? Aren't you worried that I might be able to read your mind?" she asked.

"Can you?" He grinned teasingly, setting her at ease.

"No." Though she wished she could. Then she'd be able to find out why he was being so nice to her and why he'd offered to protect her.

"Actually, I think it's impressive," Phelan said.

"Why?" She picked up her sandwich and took another bite.

"I thought empaths felt the emotions and energies of others. It has to be tough working around a lot of people all the time."

Yes, it was, but she'd learned a long time ago how to control or block the emotions from becoming debilitating. Most of the time, it wasn't a problem. Only on rare occasions, when there were too many people around or she was exhausted, was it hard to maintain the barrier without experiencing some pain. "It's a lot harder in smaller spaces. At the casino, I can move around, distance myself if it becomes overwhelming."

She'd tried working in an office once, and the job had lasted only a couple of weeks. Besides her wolf feeling trapped, she had nowhere to go if any of her coworkers got extremely upset. She'd have to spend hours at a desk enduring the emotional onslaught.

"Is that why you don't like enclosed spaces?" He pushed his plate aside and took a drink.

"Mostly." Tessa didn't like the direction the

conversation was going. Him knowing she couldn't shift was different from openly discussing it with him. It wasn't like they were in a relationship or had a future together, but she'd discovered she liked him. He made her feel comfortable, special, and selfish or not, she wanted to enjoy it for a little bit longer.

A discussion about her wolf would ruin it and change the way he viewed her. She wasn't willing to take the risk. If she saw the same condescending expression she'd witnessed on others, it would destroy her and she'd have to leave.

"Thanks for lunch." Tessa stretched, her fake yawn turning into a real one. "You said something about a tour and possibly some sleep?"

Tessa jolted awake and found herself in an unfamiliar bed. It took her a few seconds to realize she'd fallen asleep in one of Phelan's three guest rooms after he'd shown her around his house.

Though Tessa thought the four upstairs bedrooms seemed a bit much for a single guy, she loved the layout of his impressive home. The lower level was open and spacious. He hadn't done much in the way of decorating, yet the place had a warm, appealing quality. There was a sliding glass door leading to a nicely manicured backyard containing a pool and a spectacular view of the nearby mountains.

Her wolf vision quickly adjusted to the darkness, and she climbed off the bed and headed for the hallway. When she reached the bottom of the stairs, she noticed a light was on in the kitchen. She padded across the cool, tiled floor, expecting to find Phelan, not an empty room. Glancing around, she spotted a piece of paper taped to the center island with a note scrawled in black ink.

"Went for a run. Make yourself at home. Be back soon."

Well, darn. She felt a wave of disappointment and loss at his absence. He couldn't have been gone for long since his scent still lingered more strongly in this room than any other.

She opened the glass door and stepped out onto the concrete patio. In the distance, the casino lights formed a brilliant strip of gold below the dark backdrop of the sky. Higher still, she glimpsed the moon, not quite round and full, yet bright enough to form a glowing speck in the darkness.

Tessa's thoughts drifted to Nira and the fate awaiting her in two more days. She rubbed her arms against the shudder running along her skin. She refused to let Draven get away with stealing the young woman's life and was determined to find her. Hopefully, Ryland would get some answers back tomorrow on his inquiries about the jackals.

Phelan had a lighted pool, the water shimmering and inviting. Besides using the hotel's gym to relieve stress and work off her wolf's pent-up energy, she'd also enjoyed doing laps in their massive pool.

Phelan wouldn't have left to go on a run if he didn't think she'd be safe. She decided a quick dip would be the perfect way to work off some of her anxiety.

The only clothes she had besides her uniform was the T-shirt and jeans she was currently wearing. They hadn't stopped by her home for more clothes, too afraid Draven might have discovered where she lived. She didn't want to get the only pair of clean underwear she had wet. And, as much as she'd enjoy the water caressing her bare skin, she didn't need the neighbors seeing her swim naked.

Phelan had told her to make herself at home. She wasn't sure if that extended to borrowing one of his shirts to wear for her swim. What was the worst he could do, demand she return it? The idea of him stripping her naked sent flutters rippling through her stomach.

She mentally shook herself, shaking off the delicious image before heading upstairs. Even if she hadn't known which bedroom belonged to Phelan, she would have found it easily by following his spicy scent. As she passed the room next to hers, she detected the faint and flowery smell left by another female. Tessa must have been too exhausted and preoccupied with Phelan to notice it earlier.

She stood in the doorway and inhaled deeply. Whoever the sweet aroma belonged to had spent quite a bit of time in this room. Jealousy washed over Tessa. Her wolf growled, ready to track down the woman and rip her apart.

What is wrong with me? Tessa had never been this possessive over a guy before. Her damned wolf was acting as if he belonged to her and was actually her mate. Just because she'd fantasized about the guy since she'd met him didn't mean there was something between them. She'd be the first to know if they were destined to be together, wouldn't she?

Needing to calm her animal, Tessa fisted her hands to her thighs and backed farther into the hall. She pushed away all thoughts of entering the room and shredding anything that contained the other woman's scent. She told herself what Phelan did in his spare time was none of her business.

CHAPTER TWELVE

Phelan's run hadn't done much to cool his desire for Tessa. He'd hoped by letting his wolf roam, it would help clear his mind. He needed to focus on keeping her alive and finding Nira. Something he was finding harder to do the more time he spent with her. Thoughts of the beautiful woman asleep in his upstairs bedroom kept invading his mind and rekindling his desire. Now that he had her in his home, all he could think about was getting her into his bed.

He didn't think Draven or the twins would enter a community inhabited predominately by wolf shifters, but he didn't want to take any chances, not where she was concerned. Since he had the jackals' scents, he wanted to check the outside perimeter of the complex, ensure they hadn't tracked her. He'd kept his run short and stayed close to the outer wall that served as a protective barrier for the homes.

When he'd spoken to Logan earlier, he'd been informed that the other pack members who resided in the community were also aware of Draven's presence in the city. They would be vigilant in protecting the area and alert him if any of the jackals breached the neighborhood he had finally accepted as his home.

Although his decision to leave San Diego had been based on necessity rather than desire, he didn't regret the move. The pack alpha, who was also his father, had died two years ago. As the oldest son, the position should have automatically gone to him. Phelan's wolf was a strong alpha, and he could easily have become his father's successor. Being a cop had always been his dream. He had no interest in the responsibilities or politics that went with running a pack so he'd happily relinquished the rights to Robert, his younger brother.

There had always been sibling rivalry between them. After Robert became alpha, his manifested jealousies grew worse and put a strain on their relationship. His brother viewed Phelan as a threat, no matter how much support or how many assurances he gave him. Rather than face the inevitable challenge that would lead to one of them dying, Phelan had submitted for a transfer and taken the division job when it became available.

There were a lot of things he missed about his childhood home. The sandy beaches and the ocean were at the top of the list. The pool and the location was the main reason he'd purchased the large house. Being located near a mountainous conservation area where he could run whenever he wanted was definitely a plus.

Phelan reached the edge of his property and shifted into his human form. He tugged on the pair of shorts he'd left draped over the rear gate before he'd left. After punching in the security access code, he slipped into his backyard. The sound of water splashing drew his attention to the pool.

The last thing he expected to see was Tessa wearing one of his old T-shirts and floating on her back, paddling her feet up and down, staring at the star-filled sky.

His pool, his shirt, his…?

Mate. His wolf growled, refusing to let Phelan believe she was anything else.

Moving with the stealth of his kind, he lowered himself over the edge and slipped into the water. Staying below the surface, he used the water to disguise his scent. Her feet touched the bottom of the pool right before he reached her. Grinning, he stood up behind her and wrapped his arms around her waist.

She screamed and elbowed him in the ribs, then spun around with her hands fisted and ready to strike.

"Wait. It's me." Her reflexes were fast, faster than he'd anticipated, and he held up his hands in case she got in a good shot.

"That was mean." She frowned and lowered her arms. "I should have hit you harder."

"I'm sorry. I couldn't resist." He chuckled. "I'll let you punch me if it makes you feel better."

"I reserve the right to save it for later when you aggravate me again." She twitched her lips as if she was holding back a smile.

"What makes you think…" He held her perceptive gaze. "In my defense, you're kind of cute when you get annoyed." He grinned when she shook her head.

She rolled her eyes and held up a fist. "Don't make me change my mind."

"Never." He wrapped his hand over hers and pulled her closer. "I like your choice of swimwear." Phelan noticed how the oversized shirt clung to her shapely form. Seeing the accentuated curve of her breasts and the tips of her nipples was making him hard. He forced his gaze back to hers. "I did mention there were women's clothes in the room next to yours, didn't I?"

"No, you didn't." Tessa pulled her hand free and moved backward, taking her closer to the pool's edge. "I don't think your girlfriend would appreciate me wearing her clothes."

Is she jealous? The thought that she might care if there was another woman in his life had his wolf prancing. He preferred her smile to the irritated frown she was wearing.

"There is no girlfriend. My sister left them on her last visit."

"Oh…" Her gaze lit with a devious glint. "Because I heard you and Tanzy…"

Phelan growled. "It happened once, and it was a mistake. Does everyone think that she…that we… I am going to kill Ryland."

"Relax." Tessa patted his shoulder and laughed. "My brother didn't tell anyone. It's not his style."

"How did you find out?" He was going to hurt the person who'd possibly ruined his chances with Tessa.

"Tanzy." She gave him a look that said it should have been obvious.

"Please tell me you two aren't close friends." It was worse than he thought. He'd learned from his sister how woman talked. He didn't want Tessa to hear about the sexual details of that night.

"No. She hangs out with my cousin, Aurelia, and likes to brag." She smiled, sympathy flickering in her gaze. "It's pretty much a known fact that Tanzy likes to go after all the new guys."

"So I was a notch…" Phelan groaned, pissed and relieved at the same time.

"In her proverbial belt." Tessa nodded, making quotation marks with her fingers. "Would it help if I told you that you didn't stand a chance?"

"What do you mean?"

"I heard that Tanzy is one-eighth nymph. Maybe she used some of her magical charm on you."

He remembered drinking more than usual and feeling a little drunk that night. Normally, he never gave it much thought because his shifter metabolism burned off any long-lasting side effects from alcoholic beverages. "You sure know how to hurt a guy's ego."

"Sorry, I was trying to make you feel better." She giggled.

"I appreciate it." Phelan stared at her lips, thinking of a

number of ways she could make him feel better.

"If everyone knows about Tanzy, then what's the deal with Brock? Why is he being such a hard-ass?"

"She's still his niece, and it's a bear thing." She skimmed her hand along the water's surface. "I don't think it's personal. He did the same thing to Ryland when he first joined division."

Funny how his partner neglected to mention that detail. "Did he and Tanzy…"

"Don't care and don't want to know who my brother has sex with." Tessa moved backward until she was leaning against the edge of the pool. "You, on the other hand…"

"Tessa, I swear there is nothing going on between…"

She pressed her finger against his lips. "You're kind of adorable too when you get annoyed."

#

Tessa shouldn't have been surprised when Phelan gripped her nape and captured her mouth with his. She'd been so relieved to hear there wasn't another woman in his life that she'd purposely taunted him. Needed to see if he wanted her as much as she wanted him. She knew it would never go anywhere, could never be permanent, but that hadn't stopped her.

The man knew how to use his lips, and what he did with his tongue set her on fire. Even the cool water couldn't douse the heat spreading through her system. She stifled a moan when he ended the kiss, relieved that he hadn't moved away. He boxed her in by gripping the edge of the pool.

"Is your ego all better now?" Tessa teased.

His grin didn't falter when he faked a groan. "Your brother never mentioned that you have a spiteful side."

"He's smarter than I thought." After her chuckle faded, the silence drew out between them. The way he'd acted around her in the past had always bothered her, and she believed in being truthful. Since they were going to be spending time together, she wanted the air cleared between them. "If I ask you a question, will you answer me honestly?"

"Sure." His gaze held a serious glint. "What do you want to know?"

"I got the impression you didn't want to be around me, so why are you helping me?" She tucked some damp strands behind her ear. "I meant before tonight. Did I do something to upset you?"

"Why would you think I didn't want anything to do with you?" Phelan's exasperated tone didn't hide his guilt-laden grimace.

"Maybe because you've been going out of your way to avoid me for months. Then there's the frowning thing you do every time you see me." She tapped his chin. "Kind of like what you're doing now."

"You didn't do anything wrong." He ran his finger along the length of her arm. "I didn't avoid you because I wanted to, I avoided you because I needed to."

Judging by the way he'd kissed her, Tessa was pretty sure their attraction was mutual. She expected him to say something about her inability to shift, how it was a bad idea for him to get involved with her. She jerked away from his touch and hugged her midsection. "I don't understand. Would you mind explaining?"

He appeared disheartened and lowered his hand. "Your brother is my partner, and your uncle is my alpha. They've made it clear how protective they are of you."

Relieved and a little irritated, she said, "You're afraid of my family. Did they tell you to stay away from me?" It would piss her off if she found out the two males were interfering in her relationships again. She'd seen Phelan fight Gregor and had a hard time believing he couldn't handle her male relatives. It hurt to think he could easily be warned away from her.

"No, they didn't say a word. I stayed away out of

respect. If I pursued you and things didn't end well… I didn't want to create a bad situation for any of us." He swiped his thumb across her lips. "Believe me when I tell you keeping my distance was one of the hardest things I've ever had to do."

"Inviting me into your home probably isn't helping your cause." She ran a single finger along the firm muscles of his chest. His breath hitched, and she smiled.

Tugging the sides of her shirt near her waist, he pulled her closer. "I do have a tendency to be rebellious, to take what I want." He placed soft kisses along her neck and nipped her earlobe.

"Really?" She bit back a moan and slid her hands across his shoulders, locking them at his nape.

"Yes." Phelan held her with his intense gaze.

"And what exactly do you want?" Her heart pounded in anticipation of his answer.

"You." He brought his lips down on hers, their kiss more passionate than the previous one. Gripping her ass, he lifted her higher.

Tessa wrapped her legs around his waist, rubbing against his hard arousal. When he groaned, she couldn't help smiling, knowing she was responsible. He released her lips, then peered over her shoulder and waded across the pool. When he reached the stairs and carried her out of the water, she asked, "Where are we going?"

"Inside." He glanced at the surrounding houses and smirked. "Unless you'd prefer…"

"Sorry, not much for being on display." Tessa would die if any of his neighbors caught them having sex in his backyard.

"Good, because I don't share." He braced a hand against her back and lowered her to the ground under the covered patio. "Stay right here." He padded across the concrete to a long wooden bench near the exterior wall of the house. After lifting the cushioned lid, he reached into the storage compartment underneath and retrieved two large towels.

He slid off his wet shorts, giving her a great view of his firm ass, before drying his legs and wrapping one of the towels around his waist. Turning, he caught her staring and grinned.

Phelan tossed the other towel over his shoulder and reached for the hem of her shirt. "Lift your arms." He pulled the soaked shirt over her head and tossed it near his shorts. Starting with her legs, he used the towel to wipe the moisture from her skin, stopping along the way to sample with his lips and tongue. By the time he reached her breasts, her nipples were hard, and she ached to have him inside her. "Phelan…"

"I know." Reaching behind her, he circled the towel around her midsection, tucking the ends over her chest so it stayed in place.

Without any warning, he scooped her into his arms. He laughed when Tessa squealed and grabbed his neck. After using his elbow to open and close the sliding glass door, he carried her up the stairs and into his bedroom.

Phelan lowered her feet to the floor near the bed. "Do we need to worry about protection?" Phelan asked.

"No, I'm on the shots." Getting the yearly injection specifically designed for shifters was preferable to the alternative. She hid her amusement when Phelan seemed relieved that he wouldn't have to use a condom. According to Aurelia, who was way more sexually active than Tessa, male wolves hated them.

Thinking it was only fair after the way he'd tortured her, Tessa wanted to do some sampling of her own. She sucked one of his nipples into her mouth and teased it with her tongue. Phelan groaned and placed his hands on her hips, pulling her closer. Moving to the other nipple, she gave it the same treatment.

Phelan was panting by the time she reached between them and undid his towel. She rubbed her hand up and down the length of his thick erection.

He caught her wrist and growled, "You are dangerous." Lifting her off the floor, he laid her in the middle of the bed. He peeled away the towel and tossed it across the room, then lowered his hips between her spread legs.

"And impatient." Tessa hooked the back of his thighs with her ankles, urging him to take her. Teasing him had turned her on even more. Hot, wet, and very much in need of release, she wasn't above begging to get what she wanted. "Please."

He pressed the head of his shaft against her core, then eased into her. His movements were slow and steady, increasing her pleasure but not giving her the release she needed, wanted, craved.

"If you don't start moving faster, I'm going to scream." Tessa arched into his hips and dug her nails into his back.

Phelan chuckled. "The only screaming I want to hear is my name when you come."

Increasing his speed, he powered into her harder, deeper. He bit her shoulder without breaking the skin, overloading her senses, and pushing her over the edge. The strongest orgasm she'd ever experienced washed through her in one delicious wave after another. Phelan continued thrusting, drawing out her pleasure. He groaned against her skin and, with one final jerk, found his own release. He collapsed on top of her, adjusting slightly to keep from crushing her.

"I don't have the words," Tessa said once her breathing returned to normal.

"Good words or bad words?" Phelan propped on his elbows and held her gaze.

Amazing, incredible. "Good, definitely good."

He rolled onto his back and pulled her with him. She ended up lying on his chest, straddling his waist with his shaft hardening again inside her.

"Then you won't mind if we do it again." Grinning, he slid his hands along her back, gripped her ass, and slowly thrust into her.

No, I don't mind at all.

#

All the fantasies Tessa had imagined over the last few months didn't come close to the real thing. Having the actual, in-the-flesh version standing barefoot and dressed in only a pair of faded jeans as he cooked her breakfast seemed surreal. Staring at Phelan's firm backside and the way the muscles along his back rippled while he worked was arousal worthy and gave a new meaning to the word torture. It didn't help that she was wearing one of his shirts. His masculine scent swirled around her and compounded the temptation.

"How do you like your eggs?" he asked without looking at her.

"Scrambled is fine." Her voice came out raspier than she intended.

Glancing over his shoulder, he sniffed the air. Wolf flashed in his eyes, and his wicked grin told her he knew exactly what she was thinking. "Once we're done eating, I'd be more than happy to take care of that for you."

Damn wolf senses. Of course, he could scent her arousal, and he was enjoying every minute of it. "I'm good...thanks."

"If you change your mind..." He winked and turned his attention back to the eggs and bacon he was frying on the stove.

Needing a distraction, she hopped off the stool. "I'll be right back." She ran upstairs to grab her backpack, then returned to her spot in the kitchen. She rifled through the contents until she found the pendant. Tessa rubbed her thumb over the large red stone in the center, wishing Nira would reach out to her again.

"Somehow, fate has a way of finding you." Tessa remembered the words her aunt Claire had spoken to her on more than one occasion. Her father might have bailed on her, but his

younger sister hadn't. She kept in touch with Tessa via random texts and the occasional phone call.

Claire's psychic business kept her busy and at the mercy of her needy clients. Tessa's work hours at the casino were never consistent, which also made it difficult to spend any quality time with her aunt. Even with the demands of their crazy schedules, they managed to meet for lunch every few months.

Was Claire right? Had fate somehow intervened and guided Nira to her? No matter how many times Tessa played it over in her mind, she still would have taken the pendant. Now all she had to do was figure out a way find where Draven had hidden Nira without getting herself or anyone she cared about killed. That included the handsome wolf setting the plate filled with food on the counter in front of her. What they had shared the night before might be temporary, but it would kill her if something bad happened to him.

"Hey, are you okay?" Phelan raised her chin until she peered into his concerned gaze.

"I was thinking about Nira."

"Stop worrying. We're going to find her." He took the pendant out of her hand and set it on the counter.

"I'll try." Finding reassurance in his confident words, Tessa offered him a smile and glanced at her plate. "This looks great."

He pulled two cups out of the cupboard, filled them with coffee and set one next to her. "Black, right?"

"How did you know?" she asked.

"I might have kept my distance, but it didn't mean I wasn't watching you, wasn't paying attention."

Tessa regarded him curiously. "Should I be worried that you have stalking tendencies?" She'd been watching him too, but she had no intention of mentioning it.

"If you think it will do any good." Phelan chuckled, not bothering to hide his amusement, then sipped his coffee.

Her wolf lazily flexed her claws, loving his show of

possessiveness. Tessa snorted at how easily he'd won over her animal. She nibbled on a piece of bacon and absently stared at the pendant, an idea forming in her mind. Tessa smacked her palm against her forehead. "I can't believe I didn't think of it until now."

"Think of what?" Phelan held a fork full of eggs inches from his mouth.

"Claire."

"Who?" He sounded confused.

"My aunt." She excitedly held his gaze.

"I didn't know Logan had another sister."

"He doesn't. She's from my father's side of the family."

"How do you think she can help us?" Phelan placed his fork on the plate and spoke with what she considered to be his cop tone. The same skeptical tone Ryland used when he asked her questions and didn't like the answers.

She'd have to tread carefully in her explanation. Shifters, especially wolves, weren't fond of anyone with magical powers. Phelan might have accepted her empathic ability, but it didn't mean he'd be open to dealing with one of her relatives. "Um, because...she's a psychic."

"How can someone who performs parlor tricks help us find Nira?" His scowl was much worse than his usual frown.

Tessa cringed. "I was thinking she might know, or can tell us the name of somebody who knows, the witch helping Draven." As far as she knew, Claire didn't socialize with the witching community, but her aunt had connections with other magical beings that did. "I'm sure she'd be happy to meet with us."

"Even if she can help, someone else will have to do it."

"I doubt she'll talk to anyone else," Tessa said.

"Doesn't matter." Phelan crossed his arms and clamped his jaw.

"And why is that exactly?" She couldn't believe he was going alpha male on her.

"Because I'm not letting anyone I don't know in the

house, and you aren't going anywhere."

"Excuse me?" Tessa fisted her hands, tamping down her growing irritation.

"You heard me." He blew out an exasperated breath and rubbed the back of his neck. "You're staying here, where I can protect you."

"I can take care of myself, and I don't need another man telling me what to do." Her wolf didn't understand Phelan's anger, prowling and whimpering anxiously. Suddenly, the space between them seemed smaller, confining, and Tessa pushed off the stool.

"I'm not trying..." he said.

"Really? Because it sure sounds like it to me." She snatched the pendant off the counter. "I promised Nira I would help her and I intend to keep that promise. If you won't help me, then I'll go by myself." After grabbing the backpack off the floor, she turned to leave the room.

#

"Tessa, wait." Phelan rushed around the counter and clasped her wrist to keep her from leaving the kitchen. How had things gotten so bad between them so quickly? One minute they were enjoying playful banter, and the next, she was ready to go for his throat.

Actually, he'd screwed up, and he knew it. Tessa was proud, loyal, and protected her family with a vengeance. He assumed by her pained expression she considered his behavior to be no better than the way her brother and uncle treated her, and damn if that didn't grate.

She pulled free and wrapped her arms across her chest. "So when you told Logan you needed my help, you were only doing it to placate both of us, you didn't really mean it."

Now that he finally had Tessa in his home and in his bed, he had no intention of letting her go. He knew his wolf would gladly take on every overprotective male in her family if it meant being able to keep her. Until the jackals were no longer a threat, he didn't want her in any situation that might risk her life.

Alpha males rarely apologized. It went against their natures. Yet, if he didn't trust her, support her, and give her the respect and freedom she needed to make her own choices, he'd lose her.

"Yes, I meant it." Cautiously, he moved forward and gently rubbed her arms. He took it as a good sign when she didn't pull away or try to scratch his eyes out. "It was wrong of me to try to keep you locked up. I'm sorry."

Some of the tension relaxed from her shoulders, and he eased a little closer, dropping his hands to her waist. "I'm not happy about letting you out in public, so before I take you to see your aunt, I have one condition." He placed a finger to her lips before she could argue. "You will stay close to me at all times and do everything I say, no questions asked. Agreed?"

She furrowed her brows and pulled his hand away from her mouth. "But…"

"I mean it. I want you to be safe." No, he needed her to be safe. To him and his wolf, she was more than a job. In a matter of hours, she'd become important to him.

She placed her hands on his chest. "We'll do it your way. For now."

CHAPTER THIRTEEN

Tessa was mildly irritated with Phelan for not readily supporting her and agreeing to meet with Claire. She should still be angry that he'd refused to give her what she wanted without setting stipulations, but she wasn't.

Alpha males, even those not running a pack, never backed down when they were in protective mode, and they certainly didn't apologize. For him to do both for her said a lot about his character. And maybe something about his feelings, though she preferred not to analyze the latter notion too closely.

Her emotions were already a knotted mess where the handsome wolf was concerned. One kiss from the guy, like the one they'd shared after their argument, and she'd been ready to curl up in his arms and crawl back into his bed. Okay, so they'd only made it as far as the rug on the living room floor.

Still. Not. Good.

The route Phelan chose to travel to Claire's shop consisted of taking numerous back roads through suburban areas, with him constantly monitoring the side and rearview mirrors. Tessa knew he was watching for any signs they were being followed.

He'd remained alert the entire trip, his anxiety vibrating through the truck's cab. Understanding that his wariness stemmed from the need to protect her, she silently struggled to keep her shield in place. Tessa was glad when they finally arrived at the strip mall and his tension lessened.

"This isn't what I expected." Phelan pulled his truck into an empty space in the parking lot.

"Were you hoping for a small, dark room with a crystal ball?" Tessa chuckled and glanced at the Mystic Eye. Claire's shop was located between a women's clothing boutique and a bakery. The storefront resembled any number of businesses in the city.

"Maybe." He frowned and exited the vehicle. He walked around and opened her door. As soon as she got out, he entwined his fingers with hers, then headed toward the building.

Not only was Claire a gifted psychic, but she was also a clever and prosperous businesswoman. She'd specifically designed the interior of the store to be welcoming, bright, and cheery. The rows of tables positioned in the center of the room contained a wide array of books. Other areas displayed an assortment of jewelry, candles, and oddity items specifically geared to the paranormal. Along the wall at the back of the shop, there were several rooms where Claire and some of her employees performed readings or consultations.

"There she is." Tessa tugged Phelan toward a counter encased with glass, where a tall woman assisted a customer. Her outfit, a low-cut top and pleated skirt with a shawl draped around her waist, was a typical fortune-teller costume. Claire had perfected the image by wearing oversized hoop earrings and letting her long, dark wavy hair drape loosely over her shoulders.

Tessa knew the only reason her aunt dressed in the fancy garb was to meet the expectations of her clientele. Outside the store, Claire appeared right at home in an old

T-shirt and a pair of jeans.

Claire glanced in their direction and smiled. "I'll be right with you." She leaned over the counter and said something to the woman perusing the jewelry. When she nodded, Claire moved around the counter and headed toward them, stopping first to speak with a sales clerk who was rearranging a stack of books.

"You look great. I'm so glad you called." Claire pulled her into a tight hug, causing the bangle bracelets on her wrists to clink. As soon as she released Tessa, she held her hand out to Phelan. "And you are?"

"Phelan," he said, accepting her shake.

"He's Ryland's partner," Tessa said.

"Nice to meet you." Claire openly stared, her gaze scrutinizing him from top to bottom. "You're right, he does frown a lot. Though I personally find a guy who broods appealing." She placed a hand on Tessa's shoulder. "Obviously, you do too, or…"

"Do you have somewhere we can talk privately?" Tessa groaned, hoping to distract Claire from embarrassing her further. She loved her aunt, but subtle was definitely not in the woman's vocabulary. Claire was always straightforward and didn't use any cautionary filters when she communicated.

"We can use one of the reading rooms." Claire grinned and pointed to an open doorway.

#

Brood. Phelan didn't brood, did he? After hearing the frowning comment, he wondered how often he'd been a topic during the conversations Tessa had with her aunt. "Something you want to tell me?" He leaned closer to Tessa and whispered in her ear as they walked.

"No," she muttered and pulled away when he rubbed her lower back.

Phelan laughed, smugly satisfied by her reaction. He

followed the women into one of the rooms at the back of the store and was surprised by the interior's appearance. There were no dark curtains, no stars painted on the ceiling, no ghostly ambiance. The walls and trim were done in pale shades of green and yellow. A table draped with a silky dark green fabric sat in the center of the room. One corner had been constructed with a small alcove containing a counter and shelves stocked with a coffeemaker, glass cups, and condiments.

Claire shot Phelan an insightful smile. "Sorry, no crystal ball." She pointed at the candles and deck of cards on another shelf. "Those are mostly for show, though I do have a few customers who like tarot readings." She picked up a wooden chair with a padded seat cushion and set it next to the two chairs positioned around the table. "Why don't you both sit down? I can make some coffee if you like."

"I'm good," Tessa said at the same time he shook his head.

After they were all seated, Claire leaned forward and clasped her hands together on the table. "How's your mother? Is she still giving you grief about your gift?"

"Yeah, pretty much," Tessa answered.

"And the rest of the family?" Claire radiated excitement. "How are they taking the good news?"

"What news?" Tessa nervously rubbed her hands along her thighs. "I don't…"

"When you said you had something important to discuss, then showed up with Phelan, I assumed you wanted to introduce me to your mate."

Tessa shot him a worried look and released a nervous sigh. "Phelan's not… He's not my mate."

"Yes, sweetie. He is." Claire glanced between them, her certainty unwavering.

"Tessa's right. You must be mistaken." Wolves, predominately males, were able to recognize their mates. Phelan couldn't deny his attraction to Tessa. If she truly was his mate, shouldn't he have realized her significance to him long before now? His wolf, in total agreement with Claire, snarled and pawed at him. The animal had wanted to claim Tessa from the first time he'd scented her.

"It's times like these that I'd like to strangle my useless brother for not sticking around and teaching you more about your heritage, or your powers." She directed her attention to Tessa. "Do you keep out everything when you shield emotions?"

"Yes, why?"

"If I'm right, you're also blocking your ability to sense your mate, which is keeping your mate from sensing you." Claire placed her hands flat on the table with her palms up. "Would you mind if I try an experiment?"

"I guess not?" Tessa gave him an apprehensive glance.

"Each of you place a hand on top of mine."

"What are you going to do?" Phelan balked, refusing to follow the instructions and earning him a glare from Claire.

"I'm not going to read your mind, if that's what you're worried about." She wiggled her fingers and tossed out a challenge. "Aren't you the least bit curious?"

She's good. Of course he was curious. A part of him, a very large part, wanted more than anything for it to be true, for Tessa to belong to him.

"It won't hurt. I promise." Claire continued to taunt him.

"You can trust her." Even though Tessa seemed reluctant, she covered her aunt's hand with her own.

Phelan placed his hand on top of Claire's. "Now what?"

"Close your eyes and relax."

He did as Claire asked, inhaling deeply to push away his tension. For several silent seconds all he could hear was the sound of Tessa's steady breathing. A warmth, a tingle at first, started at his fingertips. It moved along his arm, slowly spreading across his skin until it covered every inch of him. Something inside him clicked. A recognition, a feeling of belonging, a harmonious chant winding its way through his mind.

Mine. Mate. Mine…

#

For the longest time, Tessa was resigned to the fact that a mate was not something she would ever have and that her options were limited. She could choose to be like her mother, hopping from one bad relationship to another, occasionally date and never getting serious, or avoid men altogether.

She never dreamed she'd meet someone as wonderful as Phelan or experience the strong sexual pull that radiated between them. Could he be her mate? The hopeful side of Tessa wanted to believe Claire was telling her the truth. The other side, the side that dealt in reality, was loaded with doubts.

Claire had never lied to her, manipulated her, or given her any reason not to trust her. With her hand trembling against her aunt's palm, she glanced at the skeptical expression on Phelan's handsome face and closed her eyes.

Inhaling deeply, Tessa gradually let a gentle calm sweep over her. She felt a slight pressure, nothing painful or intrusive, tug at her shield. In slow increments, some of the blocks securing the mental wall surrounding her mind faded. The barrier didn't disappear completely. If she could visualize what was happening inside her head, it would appear as if portions of her shield had taken on a transparent quality.

Next, she felt a prickle. A ripple of power that started at her core and rushed outward. It sizzled and crackled as if a live wire attached her palm to Claire's. Her first impulse was to pull away, to break their contact, but she couldn't. The desire to know, to see this through whatever the outcome, compelled her to keep her hand in place.

A few seconds later, a steady flow of warmth seeped through her system. It surged to her depths carrying a strong and somehow familiar connection. A connection that belonged to the male wolf sitting next to her.

When the warmth disappeared and the tingling faded, she opened her eyes to see a grin forming on Claire's lips. "How?" Tessa asked, the only word she could manage.

"Some other time." Claire pushed out of her chair and patted Tessa's shoulder. "I'll give you two a few minutes." She left the room, closing the door behind her.

Shocked by what had happened, Tessa gripped the edge of the table, refusing to glance in Phelan's direction. She was too afraid to believe it was true and too afraid she'd see his anger and rejection.

"Tessa." Phelan's voice was low and raspy. "Please look at me." He rubbed his thumb along her jaw, turning her head. Desire, want, and need, along with the possessive longing of his wolf, flashed in his gaze. "Are you disappointed?"

It nearly broke her heart to hear the hurt in his tone. "No, never, it's... You know I can't shift, right? Our wolves will never be able to connect physically. I can't ask you to..."

Wrapping his arms around her waist, he lifted her into his lap. "That doesn't matter to me. My wolf couldn't be happier, and he wants you as much as I do." He pressed a kiss to her forehead. "I'm not giving you up. When this mess with the jackals is over and you're safe, I plan to claim you."

The dominance in his voice wiped away any lingering doubts. It washed over her, through her, and summoned her own desirous needs to have, take, and possess him. He captured her lips with an intense kiss. A kiss that said she belonged to him, and he wouldn't settle for anyone else.

A heavy rap on the door made her jump. Phelan growled, releasing her so she could return to her chair.

"Is it safe to come in?" Claire eased the door open and peeked inside.

"Yeah." Tessa gulped in some much-needed air and

hoped her aunt didn't comment about the flush she felt on her cheeks.

"Congratulations, sweetie. I couldn't be happier for you both." Claire beamed with excitement and sat in her chair. "Now that we have that taken care of, why don't you tell me the real reason for this visit."

#

Phelan quietly listened to Tessa give Claire a detailed account of their current situation with the jackals. He heard only portions of the conversation, his mind too focused on the sexy she-wolf. He couldn't keep his eyes off her, couldn't stop inhaling her tantalizing scent, or touching her—brief caresses to remind himself and his wolf that she belonged to him.

"I thought jackals stayed clear of wolf territory. Any idea why they're here?" Claire asked.

"We're still working on the why." It reminded Phelan that when they were finished here, he needed to check in with Ryland and Logan. Besides getting an update on Draven, he wanted to be with Tessa when she told them the news.

Tessa hadn't said anything, but he figured she might be worried about how her relatives would react when they discovered he was her mate. Phelan wanted the males to give them their blessing more for her benefit than his own. He'd already decided that, with or without their approval, he was mating, marking, and claiming her so that everyone knew she belonged to him. Family or not, he'd fight any male who tried to stop him.

"Nira told me that if her essence isn't back in her body before sunrise on the solstice, she'd be trapped forever and Draven would have control of her powers," Tessa said to Claire, then pushed back the collar of his sister's borrowed shirt to expose the chain and pendant hidden beneath. "We're pretty sure he got this from a witch." A quick tug and she pulled it over her head and set it on the table in front of her aunt.

Claire waved her hand over the piece of jewelry, studying it with an intense gaze without coming in contact with it. Phelan didn't know the extent of her abilities. Would touching the pendant or the enchantment woven into the metal cause her ill effects?

"I can sense dark magic, and there's definitely fairy energy trapped inside." Claire met Tessa's gaze, flashing a hint of a smile. "In case you were worried about your talk with Nira and thought you were losing your sanity."

Tessa blew out a relieved sigh. "It had crossed my mind more than once."

"Did Logan believe you?" Clair asked.

"Surprisingly, yes."

Phelan smiled, remembering how much he'd admired her determination when she'd stood up to Logan and tried to convince him that she'd done the right thing by taking the pendant.

"How about your mother?" Claire's disgust was easily readable.

"She started in with her 'my daughter is a criminal' speech, so I didn't tell her." Tessa hid the disappointment in her tone with a nervous laugh. "Oh, and I'm grounded."

Phelan squeezed her thigh, hating that Margery discredited Tessa's worth and her abilities. As her mate, it was his job to protect her, support her, to cherish her. He would start by putting an end to Margery's criticisms and ensure that Tessa knew how wonderful he thought she was.

"Seriously. For how long this time?" Claire chided.

"Who knows?" Tessa placed her hand over his and glanced at Phelan. "We were hoping you might be able to help us."

"Help you how?"

"Since we're having trouble tracking Draven, is it possible to use the pendant to find him?" Phelan knew there were magicians who could touch objects and tell a great deal about their owners. Ryland had introduced him to a performer in one of the clubs on the strip who used the technique in his act. After the show, he'd been impressed to learn the man had been using real magic.

"I'm afraid my abilities don't work that way. I do, however, have some contacts that might be able to help identify the person responsible for enchanting the pendant. No guarantees." Claire tapped her chin. "If there is a witch in the city practicing dark arts, people are going to be scared. Magicians don't have the kind of power needed to protect themselves from her. They may not want to say anything for fear of retaliation."

"We're running out of time, so anything you can do to help would be appreciated." Phelan knew finding the witch would be difficult. It took someone extremely powerful to perform the kind of magic they were dealing with. The threat of losing their life, or that of a loved one, would keep most people from saying anything. There was always the possibility that they would get lucky.

"Do you think what you did to my shield will make it easier for Nira to connect with me again?" Tessa picked up the pendant, slipped it over her head, and tucked it inside her shirt.

"It's probably unlikely. She must have used a lot of power to speak with you. If she is a Druid descendant, then she draws her power from nature. Being trapped outside her body might prevent her from recharging."

"Promise me you'll be careful. Both of you." Claire reached across the table and placed her hand over Tessa's. "Right now, your bond is your greatest weapon."

"Please, not another one of your confusing insights. I spent hours trying to figure out the last one."

"What do you mean by insights?" Phelan asked, unsure if he was supposed to take what Claire said seriously.

"It means it's important and you need to figure it out." Claire glanced at the watch on her wrist, twisting it to see the time. "I hate to cut this short, but I have a client waiting." She got to her feet and smoothed her skirt as she stood. "The fix to your shield is temporary. Come back when you're ready, and I'll teach you how to manage it yourself."

"Thank you." Tessa stood and pulled Claire into a hug. "For everything."

"Always." Claire stepped back and spoke to Phelan. "My niece is special. You do anything to hurt her and…"

"Yeah, I know." Scowling, he wondered why everyone felt they needed to warn him. He already knew Tessa was incredible and could have done a lot better than getting him for a mate. "You'll have to get in line behind the rest of the family."

CHAPTER FOURTEEN

The minute they left the store, Phelan slipped into protective mode. He carefully scanned their surroundings, watchful of anything out of place or threatening. He caught a whiff of the human couple strolling along the sidewalk and the freshly baked breads from the neighboring bakery. Draven had gotten past him once by disguising his smell, and he was leery about relying on his wolf's ability to scent.

"Stay close." Wrapping his arm protectively around Tessa's waist, he led her toward his truck.

Once they were safely inside the vehicle, he cast her a sidelong glance. He'd never been one to leave issues unresolved, and Claire's unexplained words echoed through his mind, their significance remaining outside his grasp. "Why wouldn't Claire explain what she knows about our bond? Did she see something in our future?"

"She can't see the future. She gets these impressions, and the only way she can express what she feels is by translating them into insights." Tessa shrugged. "I've learned the answers eventually present themselves when I least expect it." She clicked her seat belt into place. "What's our next move?"

He couldn't resist smiling at his mate's determination. *My mate.* How could he not have known this beautiful woman was meant to be his? His wolf had known, had actually been damned insistent about his obsession with Tessa. Since they didn't always agree when it came to females—Phelan using logic, the wolf using primal urges and instinct—he'd chosen to ignore his animal's demands.

He knew there was a chance he would go through life without finding his mate. Uninterested in settling, he'd avoided any long-term relationships. He'd reached the point where he didn't believe it would happen and concentrated on his career and dealing with the darker side of humanity.

Staring at Tessa, he realized it was more than natural instincts that drew her to him. He cared about her and was probably falling in love with her. The prospect of spending the rest of his life with her, of having a family with her, slammed into him with renewed vigor, and he shuddered.

"Are you okay?" Tessa frowned and eyed him curiously.

"Just thinking." He placed his hand on the steering wheel. "You're not going to let me take you back to the house where you'll be safe, are you?"

"No. When I talked to Nira, she sounded so desperate and scared. If I have to sit around and do nothing, I'll go crazy."

The cop in him understood the need for resolution. He admired her strength, her courage, and her ability to adapt to the unknown. After everything she'd been through, she wasn't willing to quit. "I should check in with Ryland. See if he's heard anything yet." With a resigned sigh, he reached for his phone. When the call went straight to voicemail, he decided to send a quick text. Before he could tap the autodial, a musical tune rang from the speaker, startling him.

He was surprised to see Saul's name on the screen and wondered why the fox would be calling him. "What's up?"

"Phelan, my boy. I heard about your run-in with the jackals. Glad to hear you're still alive."

He wasn't surprised by Saul's admission. He probably knew about their visit with Claire. "Thanks again for the help." Phelan's chest constricted, reminding him once again how close he'd come to losing Tessa, to losing his mate. He owed the old fox a debt he would never be able to repay.

"How is Tessa doing? I assume you're taking good care of her." He suspected Saul already knew the answer and was verifying his facts.

"Yes, I'm keeping her safe." By the way Tessa curiously studied him, he had no doubt she could hear both sides of the conversation.

"Good, you make sure she stays that way."

Great. Phelan inwardly groaned at the number of people willing to defend his she-wolf from him. After the time he'd spent with Tessa, he didn't need to ask how she'd managed to earn the respect and protection from so many people. He already knew. "Were you calling to check up on me or did you need something?"

"Actually, I may have some information about your infestation problem, but I can't share it over the phone. Meet me at Luigi's Grille in half an hour."

The line went dead and Phelan snarled. *Damned demanding fox.* "You heard." He glanced at Tessa.

"Hard not to." She chuckled. "I didn't realize you knew Saul."

"It's a long story."

"I'm sure it is." She tapped the space on the seat between them. "We should probably get going. He has a thing about time and doesn't like to be kept waiting."

"So I gathered." Phelan started the truck's engine. Dragging Tessa all over the city was not his idea of keeping her safe. A rumble escaped his lips before he could stop it. He might have found her amused smile adorable if he wasn't already miserably irritated.

#

The forty-minute drive to Luigi's hadn't done anything to improve Phelan's mood. He'd frowned during the entire trip. The first thirty minutes, he'd spent ensuring they hadn't been followed. The last ten, he grumbled about not being able to find a parking spot close to the entrance.

Tessa knew he wasn't happy that she'd refused to return to his house. Not that she'd fault him for it. Alpha males were extremely protective when they found their mates, and the protective urges spurred on by his wolf's need to claim were probably riding him hard. Her wolf wasn't much better. Tessa struggled to keep her animal's frustration and persistence at a tolerable level.

She wondered if Phelan's reaction would be this strong if she had the ability to shift, to better protect herself. Not that she was completely helpless. At Ryland's insistence, she'd taken some self-defense classes and trained with him regularly. She remembered how thrilled she'd been at their last session when she'd knocked him on his ass.

Once they parked, Tessa waited for Phelan to come around to her side of the vehicle. The minute he opened the door, she slid her arms across his shoulders and nuzzled his neck. "Are you done being angry with me?" She gently rubbed his nape, knowing the contact would soothe both him and his wolf.

"I'm not angry with you. I'm upset about the situation." He placed his hands on her hips and pulled her closer. "You have no idea what you do to me. How badly I want you."

Tessa pressed her belly into his groin, rubbing against his erection. "I have a good idea."

"Woman, you are cruel." He grazed her neck with his teeth and nipped her earlobe. "Let's go before I take you right here." He released his hold and took her hand.

Tessa giggled, enjoying the effect she had on him, and

let him lead her toward the restaurant. When they reached the entrance, she recognized the two men, fox shifters and Saul's nephews, leaning against the side of the building. Their casual stance belied the wary and alert attention they focused on their surroundings. Apparently, Saul also viewed Draven's arrival in the city as a threat and was taking some precautions of his own.

Tessa had never met the young woman dressed in a white blouse and black skirt that stepped out from behind the reservation counter as soon as they entered the lobby. "You must be Phelan and Tessa. Please follow me." She led them along a walkway past a long wooden bar stained a deep cherry-red and trimmed with gold. Matching wooden stools with black cushioned seats lined the counter.

Rows of square tables with dark marble laminate surfaces and black chairs occupied most of the space on the opposite side of the room. Still too early for lunch, the place was empty except for the table Saul occupied at the back of the restaurant.

Though his fine auburn strands were streaked with silver and combed across a slightly balding head, Saul was in great shape for a man in his early sixties. Tessa wasn't fooled by his relaxed appearance or his friendly smile. His dark gaze studied them with the cunning intensity of a typical fox.

"You're late." Saul pushed out of the chair, bypassed Phelan, and pulled her into a hug. "How are you doing, sweetheart?"

"I'm fine." Telling the man she considered to be a father figure about the fear constantly gnawing at her gut would make him worry and wouldn't change anything.

Saul sniffed before releasing her. "I told you to take care of her, not... Your scent is all over her." He growled and pinned Phelan with a hardened glare.

A low growl rumbled from Phelan's chest. He fisted his hands against his thighs and ground his teeth.

Without shifting his gaze, Saul spoke to Tessa. "Does

your brother know you're sleeping with his partner?"

Tessa rolled her eyes and exhaled. There was nothing worse than dealing with dominant male shifters, and she'd rather be stuck in a room full of screaming children. "No, they…" She had no idea what they'd do when they found out. *One problem at a time.* She moved closer to Phelan, running her hand along his arm, trying to pacify both him and his wolf. The last thing she wanted was for these two to get all furry and start shredding each other.

Tessa wanted to say something, to tell Saul that Phelan was her mate. She hesitated, old insecurities and the fear that he might still reject her held her back. Walking away from a mate was rare, though it did happen. What if Phelan decided she wasn't what he wanted? There were plenty of beautiful women in the pack. Women whose wolves weren't broken and didn't have a magician's blood coursing through their veins.

"She's no longer anyone else's concern." Phelan's wolf flashed in his eyes.

"And why is that?" Saul stood a foot shorter than Phelan, but it didn't stop him from straightening his shoulders and jutting out his chin.

Tessa knew the old fox was protective of her, but this was ridiculous. He was acting like the males in her family and purposely baiting Phelan.

"Because she's my *mate*." Phelan wrapped his arm possessively around her waist and pulled her into his side.

"Mate." Saul's cocky expression turned into a wide grin. "Well, why didn't you say so?" He pointed at the table. "Have a seat. We'll have some lunch to celebrate, then we can discuss what I found out about the jackals."

#

Phelan hadn't been surprised at how readily Saul acknowledged his connection to Tessa. He should have known the fox had already suspected she was his mate and had purposely goaded him into admitting it out loud. Phelan figured it was more for her benefit than his. He suspected she had some reservations about his acceptance and would need reassurances until he claimed her.

While Saul entertained them with stories about his family, they finished their meal and waited for Ryland and Logan to arrive. Shortly after they'd taken seats at the table, Saul told them he'd invited the other males to join them, intent on sharing what he learned with all of them at the same time.

Saul pushed his plate to the side and glanced at Tessa. "I forgot to mention that Mario was here, and I know he'll want to see you."

"Really? Where?" Tessa asked excitedly.

"He's in the office. Why don't you go back and say hello?" Saul pointed toward the swinging door leading to the kitchen.

"No." Phelan placed his hand on her arm to keep her from leaving. No way was he going to let her out of his sight, especially if it was to spend time with another man.

"What do you mean, no?" Tessa narrowed her eyes and jerked her wrist out of his hand. "I thought we already established the fact that I can think for myself and can make my own decisions."

"We did, but I didn't agree to let you out of my sight."

"Relax, my boy. She'll be safe, and Mario isn't going to give you any competition." Saul had the audacity to appear amused. "Trust me."

Phelan reluctantly nodded, then watched her head to the back of the restaurant, his attention focused on her shapely ass.

As soon as the doors closed and Tessa was out of earshot, Saul said, "The longer you wait to claim her, the worse the overprotective urges are going to get. Take it from someone who's been there. I was the same way with my Janie. When we first met, I nearly took off her brother's head before I found out they were related."

145

Saul slid his fingers through the moisture beading along the outside of his glass, speculation gliding across his features. "Tessa had to deal with a lot of shit growing up, and she didn't exactly have great parents for role models. Sure, her uncles and brother always watched out for her, but because of her wolf...well, it made things more difficult."

"I don't give a shit if she can shift or not." Phelan was tired of people assuming he would walk away from Tessa because she was different. It was her differences that drew him to her. In the short time they'd been together, he'd discovered the woman was spirited, courageous, and caring. All the things he'd hoped for in a mate, and he'd be damned if he'd walk away from her.

"That's a good thing, because trust is going to be a big hurdle. She's not going to accept your claim if she thinks you don't trust her or you find her lacking in any way." Saul took another sip of his drink. "Tessa and my youngest daughter, Trina, went to high school together. She spent a lot of time at our house when things got tough with her mother." He absently tapped the outside of the glass. "I assume you've met Margery."

"Yeah." Phelan wasn't impressed with Tessa's mother and could easily imagine how difficult it must have been for her growing up.

"You weren't around when the old alpha, Tessa's grandfather, was still alive."

"I'd heard about him but never met him," Phelan said.

"No loss there. Anyway, being the oldest, I think Margery got the brunt of the old man's abuse. Not sure if she ever met her mate but it's probably the reason she flits from one male to another."

"Are you saying he beat her?" Phelan asked.

Saul shook his head. "Nah, but he was a mean bastard. Had a tight hold on the pack too. No one mourned his death. A lot of the members were glad when Logan took over."

Women's laughter coming from the kitchen drew their attention. A few seconds later, Tessa pushed through the doors carrying a small boy, his little fists clinging to her shirt and hair. Red-orange curls framed his soft, round cheeks. Following close behind them was a petite woman with a similar facial appearance and the same red-orange curls as the child.

The sight of Tessa cuddling and giggling with the boy had Phelan's heart melting. It was a glimpse at a future, and until that moment, he hadn't realized how desperately he'd wanted a family of his own.

Saul held out his hands and caught the small child when he launched himself out of Tessa's arms. "This is my three-year-old grandson, Mario." He nodded at the woman standing next to Tessa. "And my daughter Trina. She and her husband, Jack, own the restaurant. He makes the best damned pasta in the city."

"Nice to meet you." The woman smiled and held her hands out to Mario.

"Like I said. Not much competition." Saul handed the boy back to his mother.

"Not yet anyway." Tessa tweaked the child's cheek and flashed Phelan a mischievous smile.

CHAPTER FIFTEEN

The restaurant had opened for business by the time Logan and Ryland had arrived. Saul decided they needed privacy, so he had their group move to a room reserved for large groups and private parties. The men in her family sat with Saul on the opposite side of the table from Tessa and Phelan.

"Mates? No way." Ryland's dumbfounded expression was priceless, worthy of an internet posting. She was tempted to take out her phone and snap the picture herself.

Tessa couldn't tell whether he was disappointed, happy, or both. Logan, on the other hand, appeared as if he was ready to hurt someone.

"You've known my niece for almost six months. Why did you wait so long to tell me?" Logan narrowed his eyes and pinned Phelan with a riveting glare. "Didn't you think she was good enough for you?"

"He didn't know." Tessa refused to let Phelan take the blame for something that was her fault. "Claire said my shield was blocking our ability to sense each other."

Even if they had known about their connection earlier, she wouldn't have said anything to her family. She wanted

Phelan to choose her because he wanted to, not because her relatives had forced the issue.

"You *are* going to claim her, right?" Logan's questions sounded like a direct order and irritated her.

"Wait a minute." Tessa threw her hands up in the air. "Don't I have a say in this?" She glanced at Phelan, who had his arm across the back of her chair, casually playing with a curl. He didn't appear to be intimidated at all, actually seemed pleased with the direction the conversation was headed.

"No," Ryland and Logan chimed in at the same time.

"Saul, say something," she pleaded.

"I know better than to involve myself in family business." He snorted and leaned back in his chair, seemingly amused. "Besides, my boy here can take care of himself."

Phelan gave Saul an appreciative nod, then placed his hand possessively on her thigh and held her gaze. "I have every intention of claiming you." He placed a soft kiss on her lips, then turned his attention to Ryland and Logan. "So, I respectfully request that you all back off."

No one challenged their pack alpha, not if they wanted to live. Tessa braced, ready for fur to fly. Even her wolf was cowering, whimpering with her hackles raised.

Logan scratched the stubble on his chin, his somber gaze never leaving Phelan's. "Fair enough," he finally said, after what had to be the tensest few seconds in Tessa's entire life. He winked at her, then clasped his hands together on the table and spoke to Saul. "Do you want to tell us why we're here?"

#

"I may have a lead on where you can find the jackals." Saul slicked back the sparse hairs on the top of his head.

"Where?" Phelan hadn't been surprised to hear he'd obtained information. The fox network in the city always amazed him. What shocked him was the fact that Saul was willing to share it with them. His family's work activities weren't exactly legal, and they tended to avoid anyone in law enforcement. The fact that he'd invited them to the restaurant and was willing to tell them what he'd learned showed a high level of trust.

"Tessa, you remember Joey, one of the cousins, don't you?" Saul asked.

"Vaguely. Isn't he the one who got in trouble for stealing cars?"

"Sadly, that's him. Anyway, he got out of jail a couple of months ago and started dating a stripper."

Ryland shook his head and groaned. "This is important, how?"

"Joey said the place where she works recently got a new owner and he has two guys working for him. He said she described them as blond twins, big and ruthless. Some nights they work as bouncers, enjoy harassing the girls and picking fights with the customers.

"One night when Joey stopped by to pick her up, he thought he scented jackal. He said the smell was faint, and since he'd been drinking quite a bit, he thought he'd imagined it. He didn't give it another thought until I alerted the family about Draven."

"How reliable is your cousin?" Phelan asked. The solstice was tomorrow, and they didn't have time to waste tracking down bad leads.

"Joey's a screwup, but I trust that the information is accurate," Saul said.

"Is it possible Draven is the new owner she mentioned?" Logan asked.

"If so, he'll have covered his trail, and it might take some digging to find the information." Ryland scratched his chin. "Did Joey happen to mention the name of the club?"

"Said it was that fancy place, the Ecstasy."

"You said Nira mentioned barhopping." Phelan rubbed

Tessa's shoulder, then asked, "Did you get the impression she'd gone to a strip club?"

"She said something about complimentary tickets. Maybe she received one of those free invitations to the male revue they do twice a week. I can easily see her wanting to go. The shows are pretty good."

"How would you know?" Knowing that Tessa had been gawking at naked men had Phelan growling, low, guttural, and totally supported by his wolf.

"Don't you snarl at me." She shot him a warning glance. "It was last year and before I met you. A bunch of us took Aurelia there for her birthday."

"Is that the night you two got so drunk that I had to come and get you?" Ryland taunted.

Tessa glared at her brother, then nudged Phelan with her shoulder. "He's kidding. I end up with emotion overload if I drink too much."

Phelan resisted the urge to reach across the table and smack the smirk off his partner's face. "So how did it go with Marina? Is she going to help?" he asked, hoping for a little payback.

"She wasn't happy." Ryland's delight faded into a scowl, making Phelan feel much better. Judging by the frustration pulsing off him and the icy glare he was getting, Ryland's conversation with Marina must not have gone well. "Once I explained the possible connection to Draven, she agreed to do what she could to expedite the examination. Hopefully, we'll know something by the end of the day or first thing in the morning."

"How about the information from Arizona? Anything on Draven?" Phelan asked, knowing the sooner they found the jackals, the sooner Tessa would be safe, and the sooner he could make her his.

"It came in right before we headed over here." Ryland pulled some folded pieces of paper out of his shirt pocket and spread them on the table in front of him. "It took my contact a while to track down any information on Draven.

Seems he hasn't been a member of the Arizona pack for years, not since his father's death." Ryland tucked the top sheet of paper under the second one and continued reading. "Here's the interesting part. Thorn is his mother's maiden name. Draven changed his last name after the current alpha banished his family from the pack. It also mentions that his father was the previous alpha, which means Draven was next in line to take over."

"What has that got to do with us?" Logan asked.

"Does it mention why his father was kicked out?" Phelan knew anger and disgrace were heavy motivators for a dominant male shifter in any species. If Draven lost what he believed was rightfully his, especially the right to lead a pack, he'd be driven to take it back. What Phelan didn't understand was why the jackal hadn't gone after the alpha who'd exiled him.

"Holy crap." Ryland slapped the sheet of paper down in front of Logan. "Did you know about this?" He tapped a paragraph at the bottom of the page.

"What?" Logan's gaze lowered to the print where Ryland pointed. A few seconds later, he groaned. "Even dead, he's still causing this family pain."

"What's going on?" Tessa asked.

"According to this, your grandfather is the one responsible for killing Draven's father."

Phelan's assumption that Ryland's contact was someone outside of law enforcement had been correct. Territorial disputes or battles between alphas was not something noted in public records and definitely not publicized to humans. That kind of information could only be accessed through secure shifter channels.

"Do you think he wants revenge?" Phelan asked.

"It's a good possibility." Logan pinched the bridge of his nose.

"It doesn't make sense. Why go to all the trouble of acquiring fairy magic if all he wanted was to hurt your family? Unless you think he's intent on destroying the pack and taking over the territory." Phelan didn't want to think about the kind of bloodshed a war between the two breeds would cause.

"Makes sense. Jackals are strong, but without the numbers, there's no way they could take on an entire pack."

"But why come into the casino?" Tessa asked. "Why make his presence known?" It didn't take a genius to realize the discussion was upsetting her. Phelan felt her anxiety flitting across his skin. She'd pulled the pendant from beneath her shirt and was absently rubbing it between her fingers. He gently gripped the back of her neck, slowly massaging the muscles, attempting to ease her stress.

"Maybe his arrogance got the better of him, or he was casing the place." Phelan glanced at the men across from him. The all knew predatory animals instinctively stalked their prey. "He knew we wouldn't be able to scent him. He didn't know Nira would be able to communicate with you; otherwise, he never would have risked exposing himself."

"We can't sit around and wait to see what Draven will do. He might not have the pendant, but he still has Nira. What if he finds another way to extract her powers?" Tessa's pleading gaze landed on Logan.

"I'll contact Brock and update him. Tell him we're going to check out the club." Ryland picked up the papers and stuffed them back in his pocket.

"I need to get back to the hotel," Logan said. "With this new information, I'm not comfortable leaving other family members unprotected. I will also need to warn the rest of the pack."

Ryland directed his gaze at Phelan. "I'll drop him off, then meet you there."

"Good. That will give me enough time to take Tessa back to my place."

"No way. I'm going with you." Tessa shifted in her seat and pinned him with a heated glare.

"Helping me investigate is one thing, but confronting Draven is too dangerous. I won't risk it." Phelan tried to take her hand, but she pulled away.

"This is my family we're talking about. You don't get to lock me away for my own good." Chest heaving, she glared at all four men, one after the other until her focused returned to Phelan. "Besides, you need my help." The softened tone and the sweetened lilt to her voice had him cringing.

"Help? How?" He should have known better than to ask.

"If Nira is there, then I'm the only one who has a chance of connecting with her." She rubbed her hand along his thigh. "I know your place has excellent security, but the twins found me once before. What if they find me again, and you're not there?" Tessa shrugged and smiled innocently. "Wouldn't I be safer with you and Ryland?"

"Dammit, Tessa," Phelan growled, knowing she made sense and hating it anyway. Being away from her would have been a struggle. His wolf was already growling, snarling, and riding him hard to claim her. Putting any distance between them while she was in danger, even for a short period of time, would make the animal unbearable.

Leaning toward him, she placed a soft kiss on his cheek. "Thank you." She got to her feet. "I'll be right back. I want to say good-bye to Mario and Trina."

As soon as the doors closed, Saul chuckled. "Oh, she's good."

"You have no idea." Ryland shot Phelan a sympathetic look and grinned.

"Welcome to the family." Logan stood and clapped Phelan on the back. "Let us know if you need any pointers on how to handle her."

CHAPTER SIXTEEN

Phelan silently watched Marina sift through the papers in a file on her desk and doing her best to ignore Ryland. He'd barely gotten Tessa to his truck after leaving the restaurant when he'd received her text. The message simply said, "URGENT...MY OFFICE." A few minutes later, he received a call from Ryland confirming he'd received the same message and would meet them at the medical examiners' facility after dropping off Logan.

When they'd first arrived, Phelan had planned to let Ryland take the lead with their questions. Since his partner had been the one to meet with her earlier, he thought it was only fair. So far, Ryland's version of getting answers was to lean against a filing cabinet with his arms crossed and glare at Marina.

Phelan noticed several technicians having a conversation in the outside hallway. He had no idea if Marina's "urgent" also meant confidential so he closed the door and went to stand next to Tessa. Shrugging, she glanced across the room, appearing to be as confused as he was. After a few more seconds of silent tension, he'd had enough. "What was so important that you couldn't tell us over the phone?"

"One more minute." Marina kept her gaze lowered and held up her index finger. A frown creased her brow, and she shook her head. "I got the results from your lab guys. The green liquid in the syringe you gave them is a lot nastier than I thought."

"How so?" Ryland finally seemed to find his voice and pushed away from the cabinet.

Marina ignored him, and her attention flitted to Tessa as if she hadn't realized until now that she was in the room. "I'm sorry. Sometimes I get too involved in my work. I didn't even think to ask if you are doing okay. I heard what happened with the jackals. That they tried to…"

"It's okay, and I'm fine. Thanks for asking," Tessa said.

"Marina," Ryland growled. "Why are we here?"

"No need to get testy." She closed the file and walked to the front of her desk, then propped her hip on the corner. "You were right when you thought there might be a connection between the woman and the liquid."

"What woman?" Tessa asked, and then realization dawned. "One of your investigations."

"Yeah." Phelan nodded.

"So you're saying she was injected with that stuff, and it caused the green tint in her skin?" Ryland asked.

"Far worse than that." Marina sighed and pushed off her desk. "It's hard to explain and will be easier if I show you." She spoke to Tessa. "Maybe you should wait here."

Tessa winced. "That bad, huh?"

"It's not pretty."

"She's right. You should stay here." Phelan didn't want to leave Tessa's side, but he understood why Marina wanted her to stay behind. A corpse was not something you ever forgot. He had plenty of gruesome memories locked away in his mind from the things he'd seen. He'd rather Tessa not be exposed to that part of his life. He sensed her wolf's trepidation at being left alone in the small office and ran his hand along her arm, trying to soothe her. "We won't be gone long. I promise."

"Not a problem." Tessa swallowed hard and offered him a brave smile. "I'll be okay."

Phelan pressed a kiss to her forehead, then follow Marina and Ryland out of the office.

"This way," Marina said and led them down a long hallway.

"You lost?" Ryland asked her what Phelan had been thinking. "Because I don't remember ever being in this part of the building before."

"I'm pretty sure I know where I'm going, *Kern*." Marina stopped when they reached a wall with a heavy metal door. She swiped her ID over a small security pad on the wall. When she tugged on the handle, the door made a whooshing noise similar to the sound of air escaping from an opened seal. Taking a step back, she waited as the door slowly swung open by itself.

"What's in there?" Phelan had been to the morgue on several occasions. The inside of this room didn't come close to resembling one.

"When a death involves magic, it has to be handled differently," Marina said.

Phelan moved closer, stopping outside the doorway. Power prickled along his skin as if he'd stepped into an electrical cloud, uncomfortable but not painful. "Are you sure we should be going in there?"

Marina pointed at a thin, glowing blue line running along the frame. "It's completely safe. There are wards to keep enchantments contained and protect anyone who enters this room." She walked through the doorway. "See, perfectly safe." Her challenging gaze dared them to enter.

"She's in here." Marina walked over to a wall containing three metal doors and opened the one in the middle. Reaching inside, she tugged on a handle and pulled out a long flat bed with rollers underneath. A huge covered container sat on top.

Even sealed, whatever was inside smelled awful, and

Phelan resisted the urge to put his hand over his nose and mouth.

Ryland glanced at Marina, wrinkling his nose. "Are you saying that puddle of ooze is all that's left of the woman from the alley?"

"That's exactly what I'm saying. It's why I asked your sister not to..." Marina glanced away from the container, her face paling.

That would have been Tessa's fate. A tight pressure built in Phelan's chest, and he couldn't stop staring at the horrible contents. He wanted to kill the jackals for the death they'd planned for her.

"Were you able to ID her yet?" Ryland asked.

"I have no idea, but the examiner picked up traces of magic in her DNA. According to the lab report I was reading when you arrived, she wasn't human." Marina tucked her hands in the pockets of her lab coat. "What's strange is the similarity between some of the components in the green liquid and her chemical makeup. It's almost as if she was the source."

"Didn't Tessa mention Draven was dealing with a witch?" Ryland pointed at the container. "You don't suppose that's her?"

"What better way to get rid of a magical being than to use their own powers against them?" Phelan knew jackals were deadly, but this was cold, calculating, lethal. The kind of dark magic Draven was using came with a high price. By killing the witch, he'd eliminated the payment and the one person capable of stopping him. "If this really is the witch, let's hope she didn't make a bunch more of this shit before they killed her."

"I agree," Ryland rumbled. "I'd hate to think what would happen if someone found a way to reproduce it and sell it on the streets."

"Is there anything else you can tell us about it that might help?" Phelan asked Marina.

"Other than don't let anyone get it into your system,

no." She glanced at Ryland. Concern briefly appeared on her face before she masked it with her usual professional expression.

Whatever was going on between the two of them was mutual. The thought was quickly replaced by the overwhelming need to find Tessa. Something was wrong. Phelan couldn't explain how he knew, but he did. "I think Tessa's in trouble. We need to get back." His wolf was going crazy, frantically clawing and urging him to find her.

#

Tessa pulled out her phone and checked the time. Nearly six thirty, which meant most of the employees had probably already left for the night. Other than the technician who rolled a gurney along the hall shortly after Marina left with the guys, she hadn't seen another soul. Staring at the quiet and dimly lit corridor was beginning to creep her out.

Thinking about what had been under the lumpy white cloth Phelan transported sent a wave of nausea spiraling through her stomach again. Sitting in this room was also wearing on her nerves. Even with the door open, the space seemed overly confining, and her wolf was getting anxious. Worse, her animal didn't like being away from Phelan. If she were being honest, neither did she. She missed his strength and how he offered her support whenever he sensed her stress, which lately had been a frequent event.

She got up from the chair and paced the length of the room, then remembered seeing a vending machine when they'd arrived. Maybe taking a short walk and getting a cup of coffee would help. Finding a restroom wouldn't be a bad idea either.

A few minutes later, Tessa stood in front of the machine, digging in her pocket for change. She groaned when the only thing she found was a casino chip for a complimentary drink from the Fox and Hounds' bar. What little money she had was in the wallet she'd left in her backpack, which was safely tucked under the seat in Phelan's truck.

Noting the bathroom at the end of the hall, Tessa decided to address her full bladder problem before going back to Marina's office. After taking care of business, she washed her hands, then leaned over the sink to splash some water on her face. She hadn't gotten a lot of sleep the night before, and the exhaustion was wearing on her. She grabbed a paper towel and wiped off the moisture.

"Hello, little wolf." The familiar male voice, one she hoped she'd never hear again, sent ripples of shock racing across her skin. She lowered the towel and peered at the reflection in the mirror. Gregor was leaning against the frame of the stalls behind her, targeting her with his shiny black eyes. His malicious smirk made the scar on his cheek more noticeable and him more terrifying.

A tight pressure constricted her breathing. She gulped in air and fought back a wave of panic, then slowly turned to face him. Her hands trembled, the damp towel slipping from her fingers and dropping to the floor.

"All I want is the pendant." He pushed away from the metal wall and took a threatening step toward her.

Like I'm going to believe that. Not after the last time he'd tried to kill her. All of a sudden, he seemed a lot larger and the room seemed a lot smaller. She stepped back, and bumped into the edge of the counter. Tessa glanced at the door, judging the distance.

"You won't make it." He guessed what she was thinking and chuckled. "Now hand it over." He held his large palm out in front of him. "I know you have it on you." When his gaze dropped to the neckline of her shirt, she knew he'd seen the chain.

She fought the urge to clutch the pendant hidden beneath the fabric. Instead, she inched a little to the left.

"Have it your way." He closed the distance between them, his movements so fast, she didn't have time to react.

He roughly clamped his hand around her forearm.

She winced when the tips of his claws dug into her flesh and drew blood. He peeled back the material above her top button and scraped the skin on her chest as he slipped his fingers underneath the chain. Warmth surged along her skin where the metal made contact with her flesh.

Gregor screamed and jumped back, clutching his wrist. "What did you do?" He glared at her with murderous intent, no doubt contemplating the idea of slitting her throat.

"I didn't do anything." Confused, Tessa glanced at his hand and gasped when she noticed the blistering red line running along the middle of his palm. Had the chain burned him? How was that even possible? Cautiously, she ran her fingertips along the cool metal.

I need to go. Her wolf was in total agreement and urged her to move her ass. Tessa had been taught never to run from a shifter. Their animal, the predator inside, sought the thrill of chasing down their prey. And right now, because she couldn't shift, she was the prey. She could either stay here and die, or run and hope she found help.

Tamping down her fear, she shoved him as hard as she could. Her move was unexpected, and he stumbled backward. His back slammed into the partially open door of the nearest stall, and he landed on the toilet. She left him grumbling and cursing as she bolted for the exit.

#

Phelan reached Marina's office first. Dread crept through him when he found it empty. *Where is she?* He stood in the doorway and sniffed the air but didn't pick up any new scents. Tessa's lingering smell was still fairly strong, so she couldn't have been gone long. "Do you have any humans working right now?" He spoke to Marina, who was standing in the hallway next to Ryland.

"Only the security guard, Ted. His office is on the other side of the building." She furrowed her brows, appearing perplexed. "Why?"

"I'm going to shift." Phelan knew Marina understood. She was one of the few humans who were aware shifters existed. "My wolf will be able to track her faster." He moved into the office, then tugged his shirt out of his pants and pulled it over his head.

Ryland growled, moving into the doorway and using his large frame to block Marina's view.

She groaned. "Geez, Kern. Lighten up. I see naked men all the time. It's part of my job."

"I don't care." He snarled but didn't move.

Phelan quickly removed the rest of his clothes and his shoes. Within seconds, he'd transformed into his wolf.

Ryland moved out of the way and grabbed Marina's hand. "Go. We'll be right behind you."

CHAPTER SEVENTEEN

Tessa yanked the door open, rushed into the hallway, and headed for the nearest corridor. Taking the corner too sharply, she slipped on the tile and lost her balance. Her shoulder grazed the wall, and she dropped to the floor, landing on her left side.

A door banged loudly against the wall behind her. Heart racing, she glanced over her shoulder and watched Gregor shred his clothes as he shifted into a jackal.

Shit. Ignoring the pain radiating along the parts that hit the hard surface, she pushed up on her hands and knees. Before she could get to her feet, she came face-to-face with a huge, ferocious, and extremely upset wolf.

Phelan.

Larger than a normal wolf, he awed her with his power, beauty, and danger. His sleek fur was an extraordinary hue of chestnut, and his underbelly was a light sandy shade that reminded her of a Nevada desert.

He released a menacing growl and leaped over her in one smooth, graceful move. Snapping, snarling, and baring sharp fangs, he took a protective stance between her and the jackal.

Ryland, with Marina following close behind him,

arrived a few seconds later. Her brother grabbed her around the waist and hauled her to her feet. "Stay back." He shoved her behind him to stand next to Marina.

"Are you okay?" Marina placed a comforting hand on her arm.

Tessa nodded, still too shocked and unable to speak. She peered around Ryland in time to see the wolf lunge for the jackal. Their bodies slammed together in a flurry of guttural noises and gnashing teeth. The wolf sank his teeth into the jackal's back and received a retaliatory bite to the shoulder. He clawed his way free and circled his opponent.

Growls tore through the air as both animals continued to snarl, claw, and bite each other. The wolf lost his footing and hit the floor. Before he could stand, the jackal lunged and latched on to his hind leg. His painful yelp and the additional blood coating his fur was more than Tessa could stand. Phelan was her mate, she'd fallen in love with him, and the thought of losing him was unbearable. Hating the feeling of helplessness washing over her and terrified he might be killed, she grabbed Ryland's arm and pleaded, "Help him."

"This is his fight. The jackal never should have threatened you." He clasped his hand over hers and gave her a reassuring squeeze. "He'll rip me apart if I try to interfere."

Tessa knew her brother was right, but it didn't help the terror gripping her.

#

Even after he'd shifted, Phelan beat himself up for leaving Tessa alone. He'd turned the hunt over to his wolf and became a silent passenger, aware of everything that happened. Rushing down the halls, it hadn't taken his animal long to track her down. The scent of her fear and the smell of her blood filled the air and enraged the wolf. When he entered the corridor and found her sprawled on the floor with the jackal bearing down on her, he lost control.

Every primal urge to protect, to kill the creature who planned to harm his mate, overrode all rational thought. Phelan would have fought to the death before letting anything happen to her.

The battle had been painful and bloody. It ended with his wolf sinking his fangs into the jackal's throat and snapping his neck.

The wolf didn't care that he was exhausted, covered in wounds, and weak from blood loss. The threat was dead, and all that mattered was his mate. He tossed the carcass aside and found Tessa slowly approaching him. She dropped to her knees beside him. "Phelan, please shift back," she coaxed and rubbed the fur between his ears. It was probably the only place on his entire body that didn't hurt and wasn't covered with blood. Shifting back into his human form took some effort, but he eventually ended up with his bare butt sitting on the cold vinyl floor.

"I thought I was going to lose you." Tessa trembled as she scooted closer to him and gently cupped his cheek.

"Never." He pressed his head into her hand, needing to inhale her scent, to assure his wolf that she was unharmed. Catching a glimpse of the healing scratches on her chest, renewed fury burned through him. If he hadn't already killed the jackal, he'd be tempted to go after him again.

She examined every inch of him and frowned at his battered and bruised condition. "Where are your clothes? We need to get you to a hospital." Her distressed tone cracked, and a single tear trickled down her cheek.

"It looks worse than it is. I'll be fine. Most of the wounds are already healing."

"Will you at least allow us to clean you up? My wolf can smell your blood, and having the scent of the jackal all over you is upsetting her."

"Of course." Phelan wanted to caress her cheek, wipe away her tears and the anguish on her face. He refrained, not wanting to get any of the jackal's blood on her.

"There's a shower in the women's locker room down that hall." Marina kept her gaze averted and pointed to the right. "I'll get his clothes and bring them to you. Afterward, Ryland can help me move the jackal's body and clean up this mess."

"Wait," Ryland said when she moved in the direction of her office. "There could be others. I don't want you going anywhere alone. Let's get him to the shower, then I'll go with you." His authoritative tone left no doubt he wouldn't accept any arguing.

Marina flinched, drawing her lips tight, no doubt holding back a response. Phelan almost felt sorry for his partner. The anger in her glare said she didn't appreciate being bossed around, and they'd definitely be having a discussion about it later.

"Come on." Ryland grabbed him by the arm and helped Tessa get him to his feet. "Can you walk?"

"I can make it." Phelan walked with a limp and ignored the throbbing pain in his leg from the jackal's bite.

Tessa stayed close to his side, offering him a supportive smile, appearing determined and strong. He hadn't missed the fear in her eyes and sensed her vulnerability, her turmoil, and how close she was to the edge of breaking down. The sooner he got cleaned up, the sooner he could hold her and give her the comfort she needed.

#

One hour later, they were all back in Marina's office with Logan on speaker phone. Phelan was cleaned up and dressed, had taken a chair against the wall, and had Tessa sitting on his lap. The shock of nearly losing her again had left his emotions raw and unsettled. He refused to let her go, too afraid something might happen to her if he did.

Earlier, after Phelan had showered, he'd declined Marina's offer to examine his wounds, knowing that letting another female touch him would upset his mate. He had to reassure Tessa that he'd been in worse fights and would be fully healed in a couple of days.

After Ryland had done a quick check of the building and found no sign of Draven or Kynan, he'd helped Marina move the jackal's body to the morgue and scrubbed the blood off the floor. The only signs a battle had taken place were a few scratches in the vinyl.

"Is anyone besides me wondering how these guys keep finding my niece?" Logan's irritation resounded through the room.

Ryland stopped pacing the small patch of floor in front of the desk and rolled his shoulders. "I was thinking the same thing but haven't got a clue."

Tessa lifted her hip and retrieved her phone from her back pocket. She swiped her thumb across the screen, and Phelan noticed that she'd gotten an earlier text message from her aunt asking her to call.

She squirmed to get off his lap, and he tightened his grip. "Where are you going?"

"Out in the hall to call Claire. She might be able to help."

"Talk from here. I'm sure everyone would be interested to hear what she has to say." Phelan didn't care if they were or not; he wasn't letting her out of his sight.

Suddenly, the room grew quiet, everyone's attention focused on Tessa. "Okay." She relaxed against him and placed the call. After two rings, Claire answered, "Hey, sweetie. Thank you for calling me back."

"No problem. Do you mind if I put you on speaker?" Tessa asked. "Ryland and Phelan are here, along with Marina from the medical examiners' office. We also have Logan on a conference call."

"Not at all," Claire said.

Tessa tapped the screen of her phone a couple of times. "Okay, we should be able to hear you now."

"Good. I might have found the witch connected with

the jackals. Her name is Geraldine Harris. Supposedly, she lives in Arizona but no one has seen her for a few days."

"Fits the timeline." Phelan glanced at Ryland, who was nodding in agreement. Hopefully, now that they had a name, it would be easy to confirm that the woman, or what was left of her, was the same person.

"What timeline? What am I missing?" Claire asked.

"Thank you for the information, but we'll have to explain the rest later." Phelan didn't want to share the specifics of their case. Not because he didn't think Claire was trustworthy, but because the information could put her in danger. "We have another problem we're hoping you can help us with."

"Sure, I'll do whatever I can."

Phelan gave her a brief explanation of Gregor's attack, including what Tessa told them about the burn he'd received when he tried to remove the chain. He didn't want to remind Tessa about his battle with the jackal, so he omitted giving any details. "We need to know how Gregor found her again."

"I don't think they're tracking Tessa. I think they've discovered a way to find the pendant." Claire's tone grew serious. "Tell me exactly what happened when Gregor tried to remove it."

"The metal got warm when he touched the chain. Somehow, it blistered his skin but didn't do anything to mine." Tessa nervously clutched the piece of jewelry through her shirt. "How is that possible?"

"Do you think Nira is using her magic to keep it safe?" Marina, who'd been silently sitting at her desk, lifted her head. Between glaring at Ryland and reading documents, she hadn't said much since they returned to her office.

"I don't know much about fairy magic, so I'm not sure. Hold on a minute, I want to check something." The noise in the background sounded like Claire was shuffling through papers. "Crap. This isn't good."

"What?" Tessa asked, tensing against him.

"It sounds like Nira has somehow bonded with you. If anyone tries to remove it… You saw what happened."

"Can we put the damned thing somewhere safe? Preferably far away from my niece," Logan growled.

"I don't think so, not without hurting both women," Claire said.

"Is there a way to sever the link without her getting hurt?" Phelan hated that Tessa was a walking beacon for the jackals. He rubbed her back, hoping to ease some of her anxiety and help settle her wolf.

"The only way to break the connection is to return Nira's essence to her body," Claire said.

"How are we supposed to make that happen, especially when we have no clue where Draven has her hidden?" Logan vocalized what Phelan had been thinking.

"What happens to Tessa if we don't find Nira before sunset on the solstice?" The thought of losing her now that he'd found her was unbearable and made it hard to breathe.

No one answered. There wasn't anything anyone could say to alleviate the frustration blanketing the room.

Finally, Tessa broke the silence. "What about the strip club? The one Joey mentioned." She offered a weak smile. "It's worth a shot, right?"

"I agree. It's the best lead we have so far." Ryland glanced at Tessa, love for his sister evident in his supportive gaze.

"Great, let's go." Phelan needed a place to start and was unquestionably onboard with the idea. He needed to do something, anything to ensure Tessa's safety.

Ryland glanced at his watch. "It's too late to go now. It's the second night of the revue and the place will be crawling with women, mostly humans. If Draven is there and gets wind of us, he might shift, and people could get hurt."

"What about having Brock send a team after the show?" Logan asked.

169

"I don't want to risk it. If something goes wrong, and Draven moves Nira…" *Tessa could die.* The words stuck in Phelan's constricted throat.

Ryland moved his concerned gaze from his sister to Phelan. "You're still healing. Why don't you go home and get some rest? I'll come by your place first thing tomorrow. There shouldn't be many people around if we check out the club in the morning. It will buy us more time in case…"

In case we're wrong. Phelan couldn't say the words out loud either.

Rest could wait. Phelan and his wolf had something more important in mind for their mate.

CHAPTER EIGHTEEN

By the time they arrived at Phelan's house, he was moderately comfortable with the measures they'd taken for Tessa's safety. The pack members Logan alerted would help guard the community. Brock had also ordered several men to assist with patrolling the area.

He followed Tessa up the stairs to the upper level of his home. When they reached the top, he took her hand and led her to his bedroom.

Once inside, Tessa walked across the room. She removed the pendant, solemnly staring at it before setting it on the dresser. "Do you mind if I take a shower first?"

Phelan stared at the woman he loved, and a ravenous longing unraveled within him. He knew he should let her go, then join her for some much-needed rest. The sensible side of his brain battled with the dominant side of his wolf's nature—the animal won. "Later." He tugged his shirt over his head and tossed it on the floor. "After I claim you."

"What?" She slowly turned, her expression a mixture of shock and anticipation.

He gripped her hips, drawing her closer. "I know I said I'd wait until you were ready, but I don't think I can. I've spent months thinking about you, wanting you, and now that I have you…" He covered her mouth with his, delving deep, possessing, owning.

Tessa pulled away from the kiss, panting. "What if you change your mind?"

In the short time they'd spent together, he'd witnessed her strength on numerous levels, yet in this one thing, she still expressed doubts. Doubts he planned to permanently wash away. "Only a fool would give up someone as special as you. You're my mate, and there is no way I'm going to change my mind." He tightened his hold on her hair, tilting her head, exposing the length of her neck. He lowered his head, licking and tasting as he left a trail of kisses across her soft skin.

She whimpered and gripped his shoulders, giving herself over to his demands. Groaning, he wrapped an arm around her waist and pulled her snug against his straining erection. Molten heat rushed through him, along with the need to be inside her. Phelan knew there would be no taking his time, no passionate seduction. His wolf would not be denied. The animal rode him hard, demanding that he sink his teeth into her flesh and mark what belonged to him.

Releasing her, he stepped back. "Take off your clothes." He restrained the impulse to rip the material from her body. The choice to continue, to accept him, had to be hers. She bit her lower lip, her desire filled gaze never leaving his as she unbuttoned her shirt and stripped naked for him.

The remainder of his clothes quickly joined the pile on the floor. "You're sure?"

"Yes." Stepping into him, she sucked his nipple into her mouth and nipped it with her teeth. At the same time, she ran her fingers along his chest, grazing his abs with her nails.

A rumble tore from Phelan's chest. He pulled her into his arms and captured her mouth. The scent of her arousal teased his senses, letting him know she was wet and ready for him. "I can't wait any longer."

"Then don't." She ground against him, sending another surge of heat straight to his groin.

He walked her backward, then turned her around so she was facing the bed and her back was against his chest. He lifted her off the floor, setting her on the bed so she was on her hands and knees. "Scoot forward."

She moved to the middle of the bed, spreading her legs to make room for him to kneel between them. Glancing over her shoulder, she flashed him a teasing smile. "Like this?"

"Perfect." *Exquisite.* He admired her phenomenal backside as he crawled on the bed behind her.

Framing her with his larger body, he enjoyed the feel of her warm skin pressing against his chest. He pushed aside her hair, nuzzling her neck and licking the spot he intended to mark. He grinned against her skin when she shivered. "You're mine, Tessa. Never forget that." Lining himself up with her core, he plunged hard and deep.

"Yes," she gasped and rocked back to meet his thrust.

Maintaining what little control he had left, he moved in and out of her slowly. He wanted this to be good for her, to draw out her pleasure as long as possible.

She dug her nails into the comforter and squirmed against him. "Please, faster. I need to come."

Who was he to deny his she-wolf what she wanted? Shifting his weight, he braced on one arm. He gripped her hip, then increased his speed and pounded into her. She moaned, her body tightened around him, and he knew she was close. Several more deep thrusts and her climax hit. She screamed his name and shuddered beneath him.

He fisted his hand in her hair to hold her in place. "Mine," he growled and sank his teeth into her shoulder. With a final thrust, his release tore through him, an intense and mind-shattering wave of ecstasy.

Seconds later, Tessa dropped to the bed, and Phelan

collapsed on top of her, adjusting his weight to keep from crushing her. "Are you okay?" He panted and licked the blood from her wound.

"Amazing," she managed through heavy gasps.

I couldn't agree more. He rolled on his side and pulled her against his chest. "Good, because I plan to do it again, and often."

"Mmm, I like that plan." She snuggled closer.

Sated and content that she was finally his, he pressed a kiss to the back of her head and closed his eyes. Tomorrow, they'd tackle the problem with the jackals.

Together.

#

Tessa sat on a stool in the kitchen and glared at her brother, unable to muster even an ounce of love for the man. When Ryland had said first thing in the morning, she thought he meant some time before noon. Not ten minutes after the sun came up. She knew they were running out of time, and he was concerned for her welfare. It was way too early to take those things into consideration.

The object of her contempt strolled around the counter and poured himself a cup of coffee. "What happened to getting some rest?" He smirked, glancing from her to Phelan, who wore a murderous frown and didn't appear happy either.

Apparently, Ryland found it humorous to jolt them out of bed by incessantly ringing the doorbell and hollering for them to get up. She hadn't showered, had barely managed to pull on one of Phelan's T-shirts, and hadn't had any coffee yet. *Yep, definitely going to kill him.*

Tessa had to admit her mate was handsome with his hair mussed and wearing nothing but a pair of sweatpants. Phelan had kept his promise at least three times during the night, and she inwardly smiled. It was the reason they hadn't gotten more than a few hours of sleep.

Ryland sniffed the air and approached Tessa. "You are so close to losing body parts." She groaned and slapped at his hand when he tugged the edge of her shirt back to expose the partially healed bite on her shoulder. Phelan had bitten her hard enough to leave a permanent scar, proof that she was taken, and a warning to other males.

"Congratulations." He kissed the top of her head and nodded at Phelan.

"Thanks." Phelan returned the gesture, his frown slowly fading.

"Why don't you both get cleaned up, and I'll cook breakfast." Ryland didn't wait for an answer before rifling through the refrigerator and setting containers on the counter. "Afterward, we'll see about hunting some jackals." He flashed them a wide smile. "Brock received confirmation that Draven bought the Ecstasy."

After what happened with Gregor, Phelan wasn't willing to let her out of his sight. Tessa sat in the front seat of his truck, snugly wedged between him and Ryland. He'd parked in a secluded spot of a lot half a block away from the Ecstasy Club. They had full view of the front door and the entrance to the alley that ran behind the building.

There were a few people strolling along the sidewalks, standing around chatting, or heading into one of the handful of casinos lining the street. Surprisingly, the club appeared to be closed. No one had entered or left in the twenty minutes they'd been watching the building.

"I think we've waited long enough." Ryland opened the door and exited the vehicle.

Phelan did the same. Tessa scooted across his seat and was ready to get out when Phelan blocked the doorway. "Where do you think you're going?"

"With you."

"You're staying in the truck." Concern hardened his expression.

"I thought we were past the whole controlling thing." She gritted her teeth and tried to slide past him.

"We are." He braced his hands on the frame and softened his voice. "At least wait until we've had a chance to make sure it's safe. Then you can come in."

She didn't like the idea of being left behind or being separated from him. By offering her a compromise, he was showing his support, and she'd be foolish not to accept it. "Fine." She slumped back in the seat. "What about Nira?"

"If we find her, I'll call you." He cupped her cheek and gave her a kiss. "Thank you."

"Be careful." She pulled her legs inside so he could close the door. "You too," she said to Ryland through the open passenger window.

"Always." He grinned and followed Phelan across the street. They moved along the side of the building and ducked into the alley's entrance.

She'd never been good at waiting and anxiously rubbed the pendant through the fabric of her shirt. After ten minutes, she was ready to claw something. Even with both windows open, it didn't take long for the inside of the cab to get uncomfortably warm. Tessa ran her hand through her hair and felt the dampness along the roots. Phelan had left the keys in the ignition. She'd thought about starting the engine to run the air conditioner but didn't want to draw anyone's attention.

After a few more minutes, she noticed Kynan moving quickly through a nearby crowd. She ducked lower in her seat, afraid he might see her as he rushed past the front of the building and disappeared into the alley. She had to warn the guys. Retrieving her phone, she called Phelan's number. "Pick up, pick up, pick up." Tessa impatiently tapped the steering wheel, wishing her gift had been telepathy so she could mentally warn them.

When the call went to voicemail, she fought the temptation to throw her phone out the window. Struggling with indecision, she contemplated what she should do next. If she contacted Brock, he'd send help, but by the time someone arrived, it might be too late. Calling Logan wasn't much better. He was at the hotel and not any closer.

Tessa decided it was better to deal with an angry mate versus a dead one. She started the truck to close the windows, grabbed the keys, and headed for the alley. Five feet past the entrance, the stench of rotted garbage hit her nostrils. The eerie silence and shadowed areas had her wolf pacing, wary and alert. She didn't see any sign of Kynan and cautiously entered the club's rear entrance. The lighting inside the building wasn't much better. Her heart raced, her nerves tingled, and she tensed at the slightest noise.

Picking up Phelan's scent, she moved along the corridor in front of her, hoping it wouldn't take her long to find him and Ryland. She peeked in each room she passed. One was an office and the rest were changing rooms with vanity mirrors and racks of costumes. Thankfully, they were all empty. No jackals prepared to jump out at her.

Tessa opened the door at the end of the hall. Without any people and only a handful of lights in use, it took her a minute to recognize the interior of the club. A long bar ran along the wall on the opposite side of a large, curtained stage. The middle of the room was filled with small tables encircled with half-back leather chairs and two dancing platforms.

Making her way past the tables near the bar, she glanced back and forth, watching for any sign of movement.

A low, guttural snarl behind her startled her and she froze. "Where's my brother, bitch?"

She slowly turned and spotted Kynan, partially shifted, squatting on one of the platforms ready to pounce on her. Knowing it would encourage his predatory instinct to attack, Tessa bit back the urge to scream. "I don't know."

"You're lying." He leaped, landing a few feet away from her. "I can smell it in your fear."

She didn't know what Ryland had done with Gregor. He had the fear part right. Her hands were trembling. She glanced around, searching for anything she could use as a weapon, and spotted a row of bottles, capped with pour spouts, sitting on the other side of the bar.

Kynan moved toward her, uncurling his fists and exposing his claws. "I'm going to enjoy making you bleed before I rip out your throat and take the pendant from around your neck."

Too terrified to hold it back, she screamed. She leaned across the counter and grabbed the nearest glass container. At the same time he lunged, she stepped back and swung as hard as she could. The end of the bottle shattered when she connected with his skull, the dark liquid inside splashing across his face and hair. The smell of blood and whiskey filled the air. He lurched sideways, colliding with the nearest chair and landing on a table.

Her hands were shaking so badly, she dropped what was left of the bottle. Too afraid to touch him, to see if she'd killed him, she remained frozen in place. Strong arms wrapped around her from behind, and she was pulled tight against a firm chest. Thinking Draven had found her, she screamed and struggled until she heard Phelan's soothing voice. "Tessa, it's me."

Gulping in air, she inhaled his scent and immediately relaxed.

"What are you doing here?" He turned her around, his gaze filled with anger and worry. "I thought we agreed you'd wait for me in the truck."

"I saw Kynan go into the alley and tried to call, but you didn't answer." She fisted her hands and fought to maintain her composure. Her emotions were frayed, and she was barely keeping her shield in place. One wrong word from him and she'd fall apart. "I love you, and I didn't know what else to do." She blinked back the tears threatening to fall. "This is your fault, so don't you dare get mad at me."

"I'm so sorry. Come here." He pulled her into his arms and held her head against his chest. "I love you too." He kissed the top of her head and rubbed her back.

"You do?" She hoped in time he'd grow to care for her as much as she cared for him. Tipping her head back, her heart nearly melted when she saw the sincerity in his intense gaze. "Yes. From the moment you hit me with the lamp." He swiped the tear from her cheek with his thumb. "I guess you could say it knocked some sense into me."

She smiled, then remembered the reason they were here. Glancing around, she realized she hadn't seen any sign of her brother. "Where's Ryland?"

"We split up. He's checking the floor above this one." Phelan walked over to Kynan's unmoving form and checked his neck for a pulse.

"Is he dead?" Tessa had never taken a life before, and it bothered her to think she might have killed him.

"Don't worry. He's still alive." Phelan yanked him off the table and dragged him toward the bar. He retrieved a pair of handcuffs out of his back pocket and attached one link to the shiny gold bar running along the base of the counter.

"Lucky for you." She heard Draven's voice right before he grabbed her from behind and clutched her throat, his claws pressing sharply against her skin.

#

Phelan glared at the sharp claws Draven had pressed against Tessa's throat. He slowly got to his feet, fighting the urge to rip the jackal to shreds. He was furious that he hadn't scented or heard his approach. Otherwise, he'd never have gotten near Tessa.

"Let her go." Phelan didn't want to give him any reason to harm her and kept his hands away from his sides.

He wished he'd had time to get them on Kynan's wrist before Draven arrived. His handcuffs were specially designed to restrain shifters. It would have meant one less jackal to deal with.

"Not going to happen. I want the pendant."

"I don't have it," Phelan said.

"No, but Tessa does, don't you?" Draven used his free hand to peel back the collar of her shirt and expose the chain. He skimmed his hand over the metal surface as if he knew touching it would burn him.

Damn, Phelan had been counting on the distraction to get Tessa away from Draven.

"Don't look so surprised. I learned a few things from the witch who enchanted the pendant before I killed her." Draven smirked. "Nira bonded with you the other night at the casino, didn't she, little wolf?" He rubbed the side of his face against Tessa's cheek.

Phelan growled and moved forward.

"Don't," Draven hissed and squeezed Tessa's neck enough to cause her to whimper. "Not if you want her to keep breathing. Move back."

Phelan took several steps back and glanced at Tessa, glad to see anger rather than fear. He needed her to remain strong if they had any hope of getting out of this mess.

"Keep going." Draven pushed Tessa forward until they were standing next to Kynan. "Wake up." Draven kicked him in the side.

Kynan groaned, opened his eyes, and reached for the cut on his head. He spotted Phelan and snarled.

"Nice of you to join us," Draven snarled. "Now get up."

Kynan rolled on his side and used a barstool to get to his feet. He faced Draven and held out his blood-covered hand. "Tell me you're going to let me kill her."

"I think I'll hang on to her for a little longer. I need someone to assist me with the blood ritual," Draven said.

"No!" Phelan tensed and fisted his hands. Blood rituals

didn't require assistance, they required a sacrifice. "Take me instead."

"Sorry, you're not a Kern." Draven's voice lacked disappointment. "Besides, I can't think of a more fitting revenge than using the granddaughter of the man responsible for stealing my territory from me."

I was right. This was about getting back what he'd lost.

Kynan glared at Phelan. "It's too bad we don't have any more of the green elixir. It would have been fun to watch you go crazy while it fried your brain."

"There's a gun hidden inside the cabinet behind the bar." Draven spoke to Kynan. "Take him outside the city and get rid of him."

"Please, no." Tessa squirmed to get away from Draven, causing his claws to cut into her flesh.

The scent of her blood was driving Phelan's wolf into a frenzy, pushing for a shift. He needed to calm her to get his animal to back off so he could remain in his human form. "Tessa, I need you to stop." He used his commanding alpha voice to get her attention. Once she stopped struggling, he lowered his tone. "It will be all right. I promise."

Tears trickled down her cheeks, and she nodded. "Okay."

"Enough. Get him out of here." Draven turned to Kynan, who'd retrieved the gun and was standing next to him. "We'll be upstairs."

Damn it, Kern. Where are you? Phelan thought his chest was going to explode as he helplessly watched Draven force Tessa toward the opposite end of the room.

"You heard him. Let's go." Kynan pointed the weapon at Phelan. "Head for the back."

Phelan complied, staying alert for an opportunity to overpower the jackal before they left the building. He entered the hallway leading to the rear entrance. "You're not going to get far. Division knows we're here."

Kynan laughed. "It won't matter. Once the ritual is

complete, none of you will be able to stop us."

"You mean they won't be able to stop Draven. Do you think he'll give a shit about you once he has all that power?" Phelan slowed his pace and glanced over his shoulder. "He didn't care about your brother when he sent him after my mate, and now he's dead."

"You killed my brother?" Kynan roared and jabbed the gun into his back. "I should shoot you right here."

"We could shift, unless you're too afraid you can't take me." Goading him probably wasn't smart, but Phelan was willing to try anything to convince Kynan to lower the weapon. Anything that would get him back to Tessa.

A familiar scent drifted from the room on Phelan's right, and he clamped his lips to keep from grinning. "What will it be?" He hoped to distract the jackal from detecting Ryland's presence.

Indecision roiled across Kynan's features. He shifted the gun to the left so it was no longer pointing at Phelan's heart.

Ryland picked that moment to rush out of the office. He grabbed Kynan's arm and slammed him into the wall. The gun fired, the bullet barely missing Phelan's head. He punched Kynan's jaw hard enough to render him unconscious, then released his grip and let him drop to the floor.

"Damn, that was close." Phelan knelt beside Kynan and pried the gun out of his hand, then tucked it into the back of his pants. "Where have you been?" He noted the rips and blood-soaked areas on Ryland's shirt.

"I had a run-in with a couple of jackals upstairs. Needless to say, they're no longer a problem." Ryland grinned. "I called Brock. Backup should be here in thirty minutes."

"They'll be too late." Phelan headed back toward the club.

"Wait. Where are you going?" Ryland trailed after him.

"Upstairs. Draven has Tessa and plans to use her in a

blood ritual with Nira." Phelan increased his pace. "Tell me you're going to leave something for me."

CHAPTER NINETEEN

Draven gripped Tessa roughly by the arm and dragged her from the elevator onto the Ecstasy Club's second floor. The pricks in her skin from his claws were already healing, but the scent of her blood was making her wolf crazy. If Phelan hadn't calmed her when he did, the damage might have been worse.

The thought of what the jackals had planned for her mate ripped through her heart, and she blinked back fresh tears.

"Don't worry, little wolf. It will all be over soon. For all of you." Draven shoved her into a storage room and led her past several racks of costumes. He rounded a corner and pulled her to a stop in front of a wall, which turned out to be a door. It was painted the same dull tan as the rest of the room and was easily disguised unless someone was searching for it.

He pressed his hand against the surface, and colorful symbols appeared in the frame.

"What are you doing?" Tessa asked.

"Extra security to make sure we aren't disturbed." He shoved her inside a small, dimly lit room. The door slammed behind them. The loud thud made her jump.

"This is Nira." He waved his hand at the young woman lying on top of what appeared to be a makeshift wooden altar. Her pale skin was covered in a luminescent blue sheen, and she appeared to be sleeping peacefully. Long, golden curls dangled over the edge of the platform.

"What did you do to her?" Tessa already knew the answer but thought if she kept him talking, she'd be able to distract him long enough to figure a way out of this.

"I transferred her essence into the pendant. Her body is unharmed, merely a functioning shell containing her magic. Once the ritual is complete, her powers will be sealed with her essence, and I will be able to control them."

"You're stealing her life." Tessa dropped her shields slightly, hoping the nearness to Nira would open their connection, enable them to speak again. She almost wished she hadn't. Disgust, hate, and greed poured off Draven in waves, forcing her to grit her teeth to endure the pain.

"Nira, can you hear me?"

"I'm here."

Excited to hear her voice, Tessa forced her expression to remain neutral so she wouldn't draw Draven's attention.

"I knew you'd find me." Nira sounded much weaker than the last time they'd spoken, almost as if her life force was draining away. *"You have to stop him from completing the ritual."*

"How?" Her question was met with silence, which only reinforced her feeling of hopelessness. *"Nira?"* Still nothing.

Tessa heard the muffled sound of a gunshot, and jumped.

"Fool," Draven snarled. "I told him to wait until they were outside the city to kill him." He rubbed the base of his neck. "No matter. The ritual will be complete by the time the police arrive."

"No," she cried. *Phelan can't be dead.* She clutched her chest, sure her heart had shattered. Tears streamed down her face in an unstoppable fountain.

185

"You bastard, you killed him." Tessa fisted her hands and swung at him. She hit his chest hard before he grabbed her hair and yanked her head backward. Pain shot across the back of her skull. She cried out and reached behind her, trying to dislodge his hand.

His face contorted into an evil sneer. "Don't worry, you'll be joining him soon." He kept his fingers firmly entangled in her hair and forced her to the altar.

A silver dagger with symbols etched into the handle lay next to Nira. He released her hair and picked up the blade. "Take off the pendant and place the stone directly over her heart."

Tessa glared at him and refused to move. She didn't think there was anything Draven could do to her that would be worse than losing her mate. Focusing on what he had planned for Nira and her family was the only thing giving her the strength to push past her grief.

"Do it." He gripped her arm and shoved her forward.

Grudgingly, she reached inside her shirt and pulled the chain over her head. *I'm so sorry.* She used her mind to speak with Nira and laid the pendant on her chest.

Draven clamped his fingers around her wrist. "Open your hand, palm up."

"No." Tessa spat the words and tried to break free.

He dug his claws into her flesh. "Open your hand, or I will slit your wrist and watch you slowly bleed out."

She glared at him and uncurled her fingers. Using the tip of the dagger, he cut across the middle of her palm. She winced, watching blood leak from the wound. He set the dagger out of her reach, then swiped his finger through her blood and used it to make a symbol on the platform next to Nira's left side. He dragged Tessa around the platform and repeated the process three more times, one above Nira's head, one below her feet, and the last one on the opposite side of her body.

He pulled her to the side and released her wrist. "Stay here."

Returning to the platform, he stood by the first symbol and began chanting words she'd never heard before. The stone in the pendant started to glow. The more he chanted, the brighter it got. He moved to the next symbol and repeated the process.

If Tessa didn't do something soon, they were both going to die. Maybe if she interrupted what he was doing, it would stop the ritual. She waited until he walked around to the other side of the platform and was chanting over the final symbol, then dove for the dagger.

Draven was faster and snatched the blade out of her grasp. "You're too late."

Nira's body shimmered, encased in a translucent cloud of sparkling blue light. Draven removed the pendant from her chest and placed it around his neck. "I need one more thing for the ritual to be complete." Smiling maliciously, he picked up the dagger and stalked toward Tessa, bloodlust in his gaze.

No, no, no. She spun away and raced for the door. The handle was inches from her grasp when he grabbed her around the waist. "Let me go," she screamed and fought with everything she had as he dragged her back to the altar.

Draven spun her so the edge of the platform dug into her lower back. He clamped his hand around her throat to hold her in place. "It will be less painful if you don't struggle."

#

Phelan bypassed the elevator to the floor above the club and used the stairs, dread weighing heavier with each step he took. Draven was going to die. How painfully depended on whether or not he'd hurt Tessa.

He caught her scent as soon as he opened the door. "This way," he said to Ryland, who was following close behind him. "They went in here." He entered the first room on the right.

"I smell her too, but there's nothing in here but costumes." Frustrated, Ryland peered at all the racks.

Determined to find her, Phelan followed her trail to the wall at the back of the room. "There's a door here." He called over his shoulder and turned the handle on the cleverly concealed entrance.

Locked. Phelan wanted to tear through the wall. His mate was on the other side of the door, and he couldn't get to her. He retrieved the gun from the back of his pants and aimed it at the lock.

"Wait." Ryland tapped his shoulder. "Don't shoot. The door has been magically secured."

"What?" Phelan groaned.

Ryland pointed at the faint symbols around the door. "It could also be a barrier spell, and the bullet will bounce off the surface."

"And you know that how?" Phelan lowered the weapon.

"Thomas Shaw." Ryland ran his fingers along the frame.

"Tessa's father?"

"Yeah, he's actually a decent guy and taught me some things before he left." Ryland reached in his pocket and pulled out a gold coin with unusual markings. "He never explained why, but he told me one day this could save my sister's life." Ryland placed the coin in the center of the door and pressed it with his thumb. Thin golden streaks of light shot out from the coin to the edge of the door, blazed bright for a few seconds, then faded. He returned the coin to his pocket and pushed on the handle, releasing the lock. "I'll be damned. It worked."

A loud roar ripped through the room, and a rack smashed into the wall next to them. Kynan, partially shifted, chest heaving, stalked around the corner. "I'm going to kill you, wolf."

"Save my sister. I'll take care of this." Ryland snarled,

extended his claws, and lunged at the jackal.

#

Anguish swept through Tessa as she dug her nails into Draven's arm. She stared at the raised dagger, knowing she was about to die and wishing she'd had more time with Phelan, wishing she hadn't failed Nira.

She heard the door slam into the wall, and a loud, heart-wrenching roar ripped through the room. "Let her go," Phelan yelled, moving into her line of sight, a gun aimed at Draven.

He's alive. The relief flooding through her was so strong, she thought her heart might explode from the pressure.

Draven sneered. "Go ahead, shoot. I'm protected, and you'll end up hitting Tessa."

Phelan glanced at her, his intense gaze expressing understanding, concern, and love. Draven was right, and they both knew it.

Tessa felt a tickle flit through her mind. *"Tessa."* Nira's voice sounded weak, barely above a whisper.

"Nira, I thought…"

"Pendant…break stone."

Tessa knew Draven planned to kill her. Was it possible that he hadn't completed the ritual and crushing the stone would reverse what he'd done? There was only one way to find out. Tessa grabbed the pendant and yanked hard, breaking the chain. "Shoot the stone." She tossed it in Phelan's direction.

Several things happened at the same time. The pendant hit the ground, slid a few feet, and stopped near Phelan. He aimed at the pendant and pulled the trigger. The bullet missed by several inches, lodging deep into the floor. "Son of a…" he cursed and aimed again. This time, the shot hit its mark. The stone shattered in a rain of tiny red crystals.

"Bitch," Draven roared, his gaze lethal. He drove the

dagger into her chest, then released her to go after Phelan.

Pain radiated from Tessa's injury, and she cried out, sliding along the platform to the floor. She reached for the blade with trembling fingers but lacked the strength to pull it out. With a moan, she dropped her blood-coated hand in her lap.

"Tessa," Phelan yelled as Draven slammed into him with enough force to knock the gun from his hand. It flew through the air, hit the floor, and slid into the far corner of the room. Phelan landed on his back and used his legs to kick Draven off him. He rolled to the side and sprang to his feet, baring his fangs and claws.

Fury flickered in Draven's shiny black orbs. "After I'm finished with you, I'm going to rip out her throat."

All Tessa could do was watch. Her mate could die, and she was helpless to do anything. The dagger's blade was silver, and the wound wouldn't heal until it was removed. Nauseous and light-headed from blood loss, she struggled to stay conscious.

Draven growled, crouched, and lunged for Phelan. He was inches from connecting when a beam of blue energy shot over Tessa's head and stopped him. He screamed, clutched his chest, and staggered sideways. In a matter of seconds, his body disintegrated, leaving nothing but a pile of ash.

Phelan rushed to Tessa and dropped on his knees beside her. He placed his hand against her cheek. "Tessa, honey. Stay with me."

Tessa's mind couldn't fathom what had happened to Draven. Phelan was alive, and that was all that mattered. "So tired." She closed her eyes, the need to sleep calling to her.

"Damn it, stay awake." He shook her good shoulder.

Tessa forced her eyes into slits and offered him a weak smile. "Still think you can order me around?"

"We can argue about it later. Right now, I'm going to remove the dagger, then put pressure on the wound." He tugged his shirt over his head and rolled it into a ball.

"Let me." The familiar female voice drew Tessa's attention to the woman who appeared beside Phelan.

"Nira?" Tessa wasn't sure she could believe what she was seeing.

"Yes." Nira knelt on her other side. She gripped the hilt of the blade and pulled. Once it was out, she placed her other hand over the wound.

Tessa's shoulder warmed under Nira's touch. The pain disappeared, replaced by a surge of energy sparking across all her nerve endings.

"Thank you," Phelan said to Nira, then lifted Tessa off the ground and gently set her on her feet. "Are you okay?"

"I'm fine." Tessa pushed her shirt off her shoulder. No evidence of the wound, not even a scar, appeared on her skin.

"Good, because when I get you home, I'm going to spank you for scaring me." Phelan pulled her into his arms and brought his lips down on hers, possessive and demanding. Her mental shield was no match for the emotions he was emitting—dominance, desire, caring. They washed over her, through her, letting her know she was truly loved.

When he finally released Tessa, she found Nira standing a few feet away smiling at them. "I can't believe you're all right. I thought for sure Draven had…"

"I wouldn't be here if you hadn't risked your life to help me. The bond we shared saved my life." Nira gave her a hug. "Thank you."

"Your bond is your greatest weapon." Tessa absently quoted Claire's insight. She glanced at Phelan and could tell by his understanding expression that he'd had the same thought. The bond wasn't between them, it was between her and Nira.

Ryland picked that moment to burst into the room. His shirt was gone, and his chest was covered in blood, cuts, and bruises. "What'd I miss?" Confused, he gazed at each one of them in turn. "And where is Draven?"

CHAPTER TWENTY

One month later

Claiming Tessa, marking her for everyone in the shifter community to see, wasn't enough for Phelan. He was determined to make sure she knew how much he cared about her and planned to keep her forever. A week after the ordeal with Draven and the other jackals, he'd proposed.

Since nothing in their relationship was easy, she'd refused to give him an answer right away. She'd teased, taunted, and tormented him, refusing to agree until he had her pinned to the bed, squirming with desire.

Instead of going with a traditional wedding and taking Logan up on his offer to use the chapel at the Fox and Hound, they'd had a simple affair in the backyard of their home. Margery had been his biggest obstacle. She'd wanted a gala affair with half the city invited. Using a lot of finesse and every ounce of charm he possessed, he'd gotten her to agree to a small gathering of family and close friends.

Logan had done a great job with the reception. He'd set up half a dozen tables underneath a large canopy tent and catered all the food, including a wedding cake big enough to feed the entire pack. Members had been stopping by all afternoon to congratulate them.

Phelan relaxed back in his chair, crossing his legs at his ankles, and watched Tessa with Mario. Her laughter filled the air as she tried to get her long hair out of his tiny fist and hand him back to Trina. She'd make a wonderful mother, and he couldn't wait to convince her to start a family of their own. Thinking about how he'd accomplish the task made him hard.

"Why the devilish grin?" Tessa asked, taking the chair next to him. "Care to share?"

"Sure, I'd love to share." He lifted her out of the chair and onto his lap, her thigh pressing against his erection.

"Oh." She giggled and draped her arm behind his neck. "Sharing will have to wait until after our guests leave."

He groaned and kissed her chin. "We could sneak upstairs. I don't think anyone would notice."

"With their enhanced senses, trust me, they'll notice." She laughed and glanced across the yard. "I meant to ask, is there something wrong with Ryland?"

"Why?"

"He doesn't look like he's having a good time."

He peered over her shoulder and saw Ryland standing by himself next to the house, frowning and drinking a beer. Phelan followed the direction of his glare and spotted Marina talking and laughing with Vince. "No idea." He nuzzled her neck, figuring it was safer not to get involved where those two were concerned.

"Phelan. Tessa." He heard Brock's voice and groaned. The relationship with his boss had improved. He no longer received crappy assignments, but it didn't mean he wanted to spend time with him. Phelan also didn't appreciate the interruption and thought about growling until he saw Nira and an older man who possessed the same golden hair and similar features standing behind him.

"I'm so glad you could make it." Tessa climbed off his

lap and hugged Nira.

Brock addressed the man. "Let me know when you are ready to leave, and I'll take you back to the hotel."

"Thank you." The man inclined his head, then returned his attention to Tessa.

"This is my father, Theron." Nira stepped aside to make room for the man behind her.

"It's a pleasure to meet you." Phelan stood next to Tessa, wrapping his arm around her waist.

"We wanted to congratulate you on your vows and give you a gift." Theron held out his hands to Tessa. "May I?"

"It's not necessary." Fairy gifts usually came with a price, and most of the time, the cost wasn't cheap. Protective of his mate, Phelan reached for Tessa's hand before Theron could touch her.

Theron glanced at him as if he knew exactly what he'd been thinking. "There is no repayment, no debt owed. You have my word."

Not entirely convinced, Phelan reluctantly allowed him to clasp Tessa's hand. After several seconds, Theron turned to Nira. "You were right."

"Right about what?" Tessa asked, sounding concerned.

"Your wolf sleeps," Theron said.

"What does that mean?" Phelan rubbed her back, sensing her anxiety. She was sensitive about her inability to transform into her animal, and he wasn't thrilled that the elder fairy was upsetting his mate.

"It means you are unable to shift. If you will allow me, I'd like to free your animal." Theron squeezed Tessa's hand. "It is the least I can do to thank you for saving my daughter's life."

She glanced at Phelan, beaming with excitement. "Yes. The answer is yes."

Phelan stood outside the perimeter fence of his property, enjoying the cool breeze on his bare skin and watching Tessa remove the last of her clothes. It was nearing midnight, and all their guests had finally gone home. She'd made him promise not to say a word to anyone about Theron's present until they were certain she could shift.

"What if it doesn't work?" She glanced at him expectantly.

"I love you." He pulled her into his arms. "It didn't matter before and it doesn't matter now." He gave her naked rear a hard squeeze.

"Ow." She smacked his shoulder and laughed. "What is it with you and my backside?"

"It's a perfect fit for my hands." Already hard, he squeezed again and ground against her.

Tessa laughed. "I can see where this is going." She pulled out of his grip. "We need to get back to business. Tell me what I need to do."

Phelan met her insistent gaze. This was important to Tessa, and he'd do anything to support her. "Relax and concentrate on releasing control to your wolf. She'll do the rest."

"Okay." She closed her eyes and inhaled deeply.

Phelan knew fairies existed, but he'd never actually met any until they'd rescued Nira. The magical beings kept their existence hidden and even more of a secret than the shifters. Until their conversation with Theron, neither Phelan nor Tessa had any idea her wolf's failure to shift could be corrected with magic.

Nira had also explained that only an elder fairy like her father possessed the level of power required to release Tessa's wolf; otherwise, she would have performed the enchantment herself.

Phelan had been surprised by the simplicity of the ceremony. There was no chanting, no long ritual, no bloodletting. Theron simply grasped Tessa's hands and said a few words in a language Phelan had never heard before. Afterward, Theron had assured her when she was ready to shift, Tessa's wolf would be more than willing to comply.

Phelan was still a little skeptical. He wasn't familiar with fairy magic, and hoped the enchantment Theron had used on Tessa worked. He liked the elder fairy, had no reason to doubt him, but didn't want to see Tessa get hurt. He'd hate to have to go after Theron if he purposely caused his mate any pain.

He could sense her nervousness and pressed up against her back. "Let me see if I can help." Phelan brushed aside her hair, then placed gentle kisses along her shoulder. When he reached the claiming mark, he gave it a long swipe with his tongue. She gasped, and a minute later, he was staring down at her wolf.

It actually worked. The animal had smoky gray eyes, and her shiny dark brown coat had the same copper streaks as her human hair. He crouched in front of her and stroked her neck. "You're absolutely beautiful."

She nudged him with her head and knocked him on his ass.

"Hey, that wasn't nice." He laughed and grabbed for her.

She dodged out of his way, then gave him a playful growl and sped off into the darkness.

His wolf whimpered and pranced, anxious to shift so he could claim his she-wolf the way Phelan had claimed Tessa.

He jumped to his feet, intent on giving his animal what he wanted. Phelan grinned, imagining all the wonderful things he planned to do with his mate once he caught her. A lifetime of wonderful things.

ABOUT THE AUTHORS

Nola Robertson grew up in the Midwest and eventually migrated to a rural town in New Mexico, where she lives with her husband and three cats, all with unique personalities and lots of attitude.

Though she started her author career writing romance, she transitioned into writing cozy mysteries and writes sci-fi and paranormal romance as Rayna Tyler.